THE COLONEL'S WIFE

Also by J. Robert Kennedy

James Acton Thrillers

The Protocol
Brass Monkey
Broken Dove
The Templar's Relic
Flags of Sin
The Arab Fall
The Circle of Eight
The Venice Code
Pompeii's Ghosts
Amazon Burning
The Riddle
Blood Relics
Sins of the Titanic
Saint Peter's Soldiers
The Thirteenth Legion
Raging Sun
Wages of Sin
Wrath of the Gods
The Templar's Revenge
The Nazi's Engineer
Atlantis Lost
The Cylon Curse
The Viking Deception
Keepers of the Lost Ark
The Tomb of Genghis Khan

Special Agent Dylan Kane Thrillers

Rogue Operator
Containment Failure
Cold Warriors
Death to America
Black Widow
The Agenda
Retribution
State Sanctioned

Templar Detective Thrillers

The Templar Detective
The Parisian Adulteress
The Sergeant's Secret
The Unholy Exorcist
The Code Breaker

Kriminalinspektor Wolfgang Vogel Mysteries

The Colonel's Wife

Delta Force Unleashed Thrillers

Payback
Infidels
The Lazarus Moment
Kill Chain
Forgotten

Detective Shakespeare Mysteries

Depraved Difference
Tick Tock
The Redeemer

Zander Varga, Vampire Detective

The Turned

THE COLONEL'S WIFE

J. ROBERT KENNEDY

ISBN: 9781998005390

First Edition

10 9 8 7 6 5 4 3 2 1

For the millions.

THE
COLONEL'S WIFE

"Only a member of the race can be a citizen. A member of the race can only be one who is of German blood, without consideration of creed. Consequently, no Jew can be a member of the race."

Point #4 of the 25-Point Program of the National Socialist German Workers' Party

"I swear: I will be faithful and obedient to the leader of the German Reich and people, Adolf Hitler, to observe the law, and to conscientiously fulfill my official duties, so help me God."

Civil Service Oath, Nazi Germany, 1934-1945

AUTHOR'S NOTE

While German ranks are given for each soldier initially, their Allied equivalent is then used. For example, *Unterscharführer* is meaningless to most people, however corporal is universally understood. This is done for the sake of clarity so you, the reader, can enjoy the book without trying to determine if an *Unterscharführer* outranks a *Standartenführer*.

PREFACE

While membership in the Nazi Party in Germany was not mandatory, it was encouraged as it showed loyalty to the ruling order. In some professions, however, there was no option—membership was mandatory if one wanted to keep their job.

Policing was one of these professions. In September 1939, the *Reichskriminalpolizeiamt* (Reich Criminal Police Department) absorbed the *Kriminalpolizei* (Criminal Police) as part of a consolidation of all police and investigative forces under one command led by *Reichsführer* of the *Schutzstaffel* (SS) Heinrich Himmler. This effectively placed all civilian police, including detectives, under the command of the SS (literal translation "Protection Squadron"). All who wished to remain in their posts were required to join the Nazi Party and swear an oath of allegiance to Adolf Hitler.

Whether they believed in the Nazis' policies or not.

To refuse, to resign in protest, could mean death, as it would show one was disloyal and couldn't be trusted. And with the iron fist of Hitler everywhere, under the guise of the police, the SS, the Gestapo, and more, one didn't dare stand out by refusing the regime's demands.

Including police detectives, with families, whose only desire was to serve and protect the public, as they always had, before the madness had taken over.

Konrad Residence

Berlin, Nazi Germany

1941

Unterscharführer Klaus Griese stood in front of the bedchambers of his commanding officer, *Standartenführer* Rudolf Konrad, and drew a breath before staring at his boots, cursing at the scuff mark on the toe of his left foot. He knew exactly when it had occurred. Not five minutes ago at the foot of the steps leading into the large house, now the home to the colonel, his wife, and their two children.

A home that had only months ago belonged to a wealthy Jewish family that had wisely decided to leave Berlin, though he was certain the story he had overheard Colonel Konrad tell was false.

Jews were rarely given options these days.

In fact, he could honestly say he didn't know a single Jew. He had growing up, though his parents hadn't allowed him to befriend any. They were staunch supporters of Adolf Hitler and his philosophies, as was he, he supposed.

He was only nineteen. He had been in the Hitler Youth for as long as he could remember, and without the book smarts for a higher education, had enlisted after graduating under his father's urgings. The very concept of fighting terrified him. He had always been a soft boy, never one for confrontation, never one to argue or challenge another. There wasn't a trace of the alpha male in him that the Fatherland prized so much these days.

He was a follower.

And hoped to never be more than the corporal he now was.

This was the perfect assignment. Nowhere near the front, nowhere near the fighting, though the enemy had started infrequent bombing of the capital. It was something he never would have imagined. Berlin. Bombed. It was terrifying, and had shaken the population, as it had him. He had believed his commanders who had assured the enlisted men that the war would never reach Berlin, that life would go on as normal while victory after victory would be celebrated.

And that had been true until August 25, 1940.

Then everything had changed, and seemed to only be getting worse.

He had seen the footage of Warsaw and other cities that had fallen to the mighty *Wehrmacht*, and the rubble-strewn streets were disturbing. It hadn't yet come to that, though Griese wondered how long it would be before it was.

He snapped to attention as the colonel's eldest son, Joachim, only a few years younger than him, strode past in his Hitler Youth uniform, no hint of a smile, the fanaticism pure within him. Harsh words were snapped, aimed at the younger brother, who emerged from his bedroom, his own uniform in slight disarray. Joachim admonished Maximilian as he corrected the flaws, then the two of them marched toward the stairs, ready to greet the houseguests about to arrive.

He straightened himself then knocked on the door to Colonel Konrad's bedchambers, listening for a response.

Nothing.

His heart rate picked up slightly, uncertain as to what to do. The colonel's orders were clear.

"The guests are about to arrive. Get my wife."

It would be a great embarrassment if the Colonel's wife were not downstairs when the first guests arrived. In Germany, punctuality was praised, especially among the military elite. The cars bringing the guests would be lining up outside within minutes, and the hostess would be expected at her post, alongside her husband and their children.

He checked his watch.

There's no time!

He knocked again, slightly harder.

And again nothing.

He bit down on his cheek, chewing on it for a moment as sweat dampened his upper lip.

Should I open the door?

He closed his eyes, sucking in a breath through his nose. The colonel was his commanding officer, not his wife. He had his orders, and they were crystal clear.

"Get my wife."

He opened his eyes and gripped the doorknob, exhaling loudly as he pressed down on it and pushed the door open, slightly. He poked his head inside.

"Mrs. Konrad?"

Still nothing.

Though that wasn't entirely true. He could hear music playing in the adjoining room. He stepped inside, closing the door behind him, then tentatively made his way toward the sound, the door ahead of him slightly ajar. He peered through the opening, spotting her sitting at a small table in the corner, her back to him.

Then gasped at what she held, his eyes shooting wide.

Her head darted up and she stared in the mirror in front of her as he jerked back and out of sight. He rushed for the outer door as his heart pounded in his ears. He grabbed the handle, opening it and stepping back into the hall as quickly as he could, closing the door behind him. He checked in both directions, ducking his head as one of the housekeepers crossed from one room to the next, glancing in his direction. He walked as rapidly as he could toward the stairs without looking suspicious, then turned the corner, risking one last glance behind him at Konrad's bedchambers.

A head emerged from the now open door, peering out, in the opposite direction. He darted down the stairs and ran headlong into Colonel Konrad.

He nearly soiled himself.

"Sir, I'm sorry."

"What's with you, Corporal? You look as if you've seen a ghost."

"Sorry, sir, just, umm…"

"If you ever hope to be promoted, you're going to have to be quicker on your feet." Konrad pushed him gently aside. "Now, where's my wife?"

"I-I tried knocking, but there was no answer."

"Did you go in?"

The blood rushed from Griese's face. If he were caught in a lie, he could be court-martialed. Yet what he had seen was unbelievable, unfathomable, and the truth would come out the moment Konrad spoke to his wife.

Unless she didn't see me.

He brightened slightly. It was a possibility.

"I did, sir, just to poke my head in. I called her name but heard nothing. I didn't want to intrude any further."

Konrad patted him on the shoulder. "A wise move. If you had caught her in a compromising position, she'd insist I have you shot!"

Griese's eyes widened, his jaw dropping, the humor lost on him in his state of panic.

Konrad chuckled, smacking him on the shoulder. "We're going to need to work on that sense of humor, Corporal, if you're going to work for me."

"Y-yes, sir."

"Now, to your post. Our guests will be arriving shortly. I'll get my wife myself."

"Yes, sir."

Griese rushed down the stairs and out into the cool evening air, the sweat that soaked his body giving him shivers. In the distance, the narrow slits of headlights approached, and a quick check of his watch confirmed the guests were about to arrive exactly on time. He forced himself to stare ahead, to focus on his duties, but his stomach was already churning from fear at the turn his promising life had taken moments ago.

A life that was over if she had seen him.

Konrad Residence

Berlin, Nazi Germany

"Renata, do you have any idea of the time?"

Konrad held up his wrist, tapping the watch given him by Reichsführer Heinrich Himmler himself upon his promotion last year. It had been one of his proudest moments, meeting the great man, shaking his hand, and having his salute accepted. He once had ambitions, and if things were different, he might have pursued them vigorously like in his youth. Now, however, he had to remain cautious about overreaching. He no longer sought the power thrust upon him, yet to refuse would be unthinkable, and to not do his job to his utmost ability a dishonor he couldn't fathom.

He was trapped by circumstance.

Circumstances beyond his control.

He stared at his wife as she rose from her vanity and turned toward him.

He frowned.

Her face was pale, her eyes darting about the room, her hands clasping and unclasping in front of her.

"What's wrong?" he asked, stepping closer, taking her trembling hands in his.

She stared at his boots. "N-nothing."

He tipped her chin up toward him and stared into her glistening eyes. "What is it?"

She shook her head, drawing a breath then patting his chest. "It's nothing. We'll discuss it after the guests have left."

He pursed his lips, debating whether to pursue the matter. The sound of a car engine decided for him and he let go of her hands then headed out on the balcony overlooking the front of the house. Cars were approaching in the distance. There was no more time to discuss it whether she desired to or not.

He glanced down to see Griese preparing to greet the first arrival, and thought of what the young man had said. She hadn't answered his knock, nor his call when he opened the door. That meant whatever was bothering her must have taken place before he had sent the young corporal to fetch her.

What could possibly have her so upset?

He returned inside to find Renata at the outer door to their bedchambers, a smile on her face, looking as radiant as the day he had married her. She never ceased to take his breath away, his love for her growing with every moment they spent together.

He just hated they had to live a lie.

She held out her hand. "Are you ready to face them, my love?"

He smiled, his eyes threatening to betray him. "With you by my side, I could face the entire Russian Army."

She took his arm and drew him closer. "Then the war would be over, and all would be lost."

Konrad Residence

Berlin, Nazi Germany

The first car pulled up and Corporal Griese stepped forward, opening the rear door and offering a gloved hand to the young woman climbing out, her brilliant red dress with its long train undoubtedly from one of the finest designers in the recently conquered Paris. He stepped back, stealing a glance at her breathtaking figure when her escort emerged, requiring no assistance, his crisp black uniform adorned with the logo of the SS on his collar, the skull and crossbones on the band of his hat as he fit it in place, but it wasn't the insignia that had shivers rushing up and down Griese's spine.

It was the blank, emotionless expression on the man's face, as if all that surrounded him were of no concern, as if he wouldn't give a second thought to erasing them all from existence should he so choose.

Griese snapped to attention and said nothing, his eyes directed forward. When an SS general was in one's presence, one made oneself slightly less obvious.

And much to his horror, the young woman yelped and stumbled up the steps. Griese's jaw dropped as he rushed forward to catch her, his eye spotting the general's boot planted firmly on the train of his escort's dress.

Griese caught the woman's arm, his steadying hand preventing any catastrophe, and the general stepped off the dress before grabbing Griese by the shoulder.

"You fool! Is this your first day on the job? Don't you know to make certain the lady's dress is safely past before you step back to let her escort out?"

Griese snapped to attention, his entire body trembling, debating whether to say something. He decided silence might be considered a further afront. "I apologize, sir. I, umm, I have no excuse."

"I apologize, sir, it is entirely my fault."

Griese resisted the urge to turn toward Colonel Konrad, his commanding officer rushing down the steps.

You're heading to the front for sure.

"While it's not his first day, this is our first party, and he's not used to such lovely ladies wearing such gorgeous fashions. Please, let me escort you personally inside, madam, and one of my staff will make certain your dress is in pristine condition before the festivities begin."

"I'm sure there's no harm done," replied the young woman, clearly not the general's wife, mistresses among the upper echelons common, though escorting young relatives so they could be married off to up and coming officers was also common.

To make assumptions could be deadly should it bring embarrassment to either party.

Konrad snapped his fingers and directed him with a glare to another car that had pulled up, its rear door still closed.

Griese said nothing, instead rushing down the steps and pulling open the door, keeping his eyes on the next dress as it cleared the doorframe, swearing to never make the same mistake again. As he stepped back, he glanced up the steps to see the general being formally introduced to the colonel's wife, and as the man delivered a stiff bow before taking her hand, he glared at Griese out of the corner of his eye.

Leaving his mouth dry, and his heart hammering.

He had embarrassed an SS general.

And his life could now be forfeit.

He was about to turn as the next car arrived when he noted the colonel's wife staring at him, a smile on her face, though it was her eyes that had a wave of ice-cold fear washing over him. For he was certain her stare revealed a fear as great as his.

And that could mean only two things.

That he had been right in what he had seen.

And that she knew he had seen it.

Konrad Residence

Berlin, Nazi Germany

Joachim Konrad stood at attention beside his little brother, who, much to his annoyance, continued to fidget despite repeated admonishments.

He's such a child!

His mother continually reminded him that he was the same way when he was that age, yet he refused to believe it. There was simply no possibility that he, a future leader in the Reich, could have been so disappointing a youth.

He reached over and straightened Maximilian's scarf then punched him on the shoulder. "Smarten up. You'll embarrass Father."

Tears filled Maximilian's eyes, but he straightened, staring ahead, allowing Joachim to enjoy the thrill he was now a part of. The reception line. His father was now greeting a man whose insignia indicated he was a *Gruppenführer* in the SS, the skull and crossbones on the band of the general's peaked cap sending shivers of excitement racing through his body.

One day that will be me!

He had always wanted to join the military for as long as he could remember. To be like his father was his dream, to make his parents proud of him as he fought for the Reich and for Adolf Hitler was his only goal in life. He excelled in the Hitler Youth, and his grades were excellent in school. Thanks to his father's position, he would attend the finest university in the country, then upon graduation, become an officer.

Six years.

In a mere six years he'd be a lieutenant of some sort, eventually making his way into the SS, and working his way up the ranks. His only regret would be that the war would be over long before he'd take his position among the officers' ranks.

Though there was plenty of world left to conquer once Europe was done with. The Eastern Front had opened only a couple of months ago. Once the Soviets were dealt with, there'd be massive swaths of territory to deal with, the Japanese unlikely to finish the job themselves.

And then there was Africa, where Rommel was doing so well.

Then America.

He suppressed a smile as goosebumps raced over his skin at the thought of leading soldiers into New York City, standing proudly in the turret of a *Panzer* tank, saluting the chancellor in his flawless black uniform.

"Do something about that imbecile of a corporal you have working for you, or I will."

Joachim's attention snapped back to the situation at hand, the SS general's tone one of barely controlled rage. It had his own heart racing with fear that his father might be in trouble.

"I assure you, sir, it won't happen again."

The general leaned in closer as his lady friend talked to Joachim's mother. "I'm not certain you understand me."

Joachim watched as his father's face paled slightly, fear in the man's eyes for the first time that he could remember.

And for the first time he could remember, he was ashamed.

"I will have him reassigned immediately."

"The Eastern Front."

His father bowed. "As you wish."

The general smiled, patting his father on the shoulder. "Good, good, then the matter is settled."

The pleasantries continued, but Joachim had lost interest. He wanted desperately to know who this corporal was they were talking about, and what he had done to embarrass his father and put both their careers in jeopardy.

Incompetence like that shouldn't be tolerated, nor rewarded with a posting to glorious battle on behalf of the Reich.

Konrad Residence

Berlin, Nazi Germany

Ten sets of guests. Ten cars. Griese's job was done for several hours, which was unfortunate. It gave him time to think. Time to dwell. And that wasn't good, not with his current predicament.

Yet what was that predicament? The colonel was a fair man. He doubted what had happened with the dress would merit anything serious. In fact, that was the least of his worries.

It was what he had seen.

And the fact the Colonel's wife seemed to be aware of the fact.

Though with the severity of her secret, and the danger it put everyone in, wouldn't she have immediately told her husband, and wouldn't he have immediately done something about it?

But what could he do?

He'll have to kill you.

It was the only logical choice. It's what he would do if placed in the same situation.

He shuddered at the thought. No, he wouldn't kill to preserve the secret. He frowned as he strode toward the side of the house where there would be few if any people there to disturb his thoughts. It was easy for him to say he wouldn't kill, because he could never possibly be placed in the same situation.

You'd kill to protect your family.

He sighed, shaking his head. He wasn't so certain. He knew he *should*, but he was never a man of violence. He had never even thrown a punch in his youth, and bootcamp had been torture, grappling with those far more experienced at scrapping than he was.

It had terrified him.

As did the notion of killing, let alone murdering someone.

Though he wasn't the colonel. The colonel wouldn't hesitate. Though a fair man, he was a soldier. He was SS. And one didn't reach that rank by being a pacifist. If the colonel decided his corporal knew too much and must die, then he would be dead.

In short order.

"Corporal Griese!"

Griese's bladder almost let loose as he spun toward the bark. He paled at the sight of the colonel's personal aide, *Hauptsturmführer* Hoffman. "Yes, Captain?"

"You will report to the colonel's office at the close of the party. Understood?"

Griese snapped to attention, clicking his heels. "Yes, sir!"

Hoffman pointed at his boots, the forgotten scuff visible in the rapidly fading light. "And clean those up. We expect the best from everyone, even lowly corporals."

Griese flushed. "At once, sir!"

Hoffman disappeared around the corner and Griese dropped to a knee, retrieving a handkerchief from his pocket and addressing the offending boot. Satisfied, he stood, then the words spoken only moments before finally registered.

And he doubled over, vomiting.

He's going to kill me in his office.

He wiped his mouth clean, then glanced toward the window and nearly fainted, the young Maximilian pointing at him, laughing, as Joachim glared at him.

With a hate only years of indoctrination could foster.

Konrad Residence

Berlin, Nazi Germany

Konrad glanced at one of the house staff standing near the periphery and motioned him over with a finger. The man approached and bowed deeply.

"Find my sons and put them upstairs. Tell them I said they've lost the privilege of being among adults."

"Immediately, sir." The man disappeared out into the hallway where Maximilian's laughter could still be heard over the polite conversation running the length of the long dining table.

He smiled, slightly embarrassed. "I apologize for my youngest's outburst. At that age, they can be unpredictable."

General Graf grunted. "Discipline seems to be an issue in this household."

Konrad bristled at the insult, yet held his tongue.

"Joachim seems a fine lad," said one of the ladies at the far end, breaking the uncomfortable silence. "How old is he?"

"Sixteen," replied Renata.

"Will he be enlisting?"

Konrad found his voice. "After university. He's made it quite clear that he intends to be my commanding officer one day."

The table roared with exaggerated laughter, the ice forged by the general's observation broken.

"Ahh, to be young! What I would give to be on the front, leading my men into battle. I envy your son. It is a good time to be alive. A good time to be German!" The general at the far end raised his glass. "Heil Hitler!"

The chorus that responded shook the dinnerware, Konrad joining in with the expected zeal before the dinner resumed. He noted his wife's hand shaking slightly, and he reached under the table and squeezed her knee gently, offering his support.

Something was definitely bothering her. These types of gatherings were torturous for her, her anxious nature continually threatening to overwhelm her, but she always soldiered through for him, he knew. It tore him up inside what he was putting her through, yet what choice did they have?

The alternative could mean imprisonment.

Or worse.

He glanced at General Graf and blanched as he caught the man's eyes staring at the hand on his wife's knee, the disdain evident.

There would be no pleasing the man tonight.

Not until he dealt with poor Griese.

The boy doesn't deserve to be sent into battle for one little mistake.

Yet he had no choice. He couldn't afford Graf's wrath. His family couldn't afford it. Graf clearly felt he had been insulted by the brief moment of embarrassment, and was of the type that demanded retribution.

Thank God he didn't execute him right then and there!

His stomach churned at the thought. Wasn't that what he was doing to poor Griese? Though things were going well in the east, the Russians would put up a good fight, especially if Moscow wasn't conquered before the winter set in. Casualties would be high, and Griese, inexperienced as he was, would likely be among those who would die.

I can't do it.

Konrad Residence

Berlin, Nazi Germany

Joachim tiptoed down the hallway, tightly gripping his Hitler Youth dagger for courage, cringing as a floorboard creaked underfoot. He froze, listening for any evidence he had been discovered, then resumed, the only sounds coming from the party downstairs.

A party he was supposed to be observing, though at a distance.

Yet thanks to his degenerate brother, he had been denied that honor, and likely would be for any future engagements as well.

He deserves a good beating.

He reached the door to his parents' bedchambers and turned the knob, quickly stepping inside and settling on the manner in which he'd deliver the punishment later that night. He closed the door behind him, breathing a little easier at having made it so far, confident he was now in the clear. He made for the window with a view of the side of the house and peered out.

Good.

The corporal that had vomited was still there, pacing back and forth, clearly a bundle of nerves. He had to be the one who had created the embarrassing situation with the general earlier, and was absolutely the cause of his brother's uncontrolled laughter and their eventual dismissal for the evening.

It had been humiliating, a raucous round of laughter having erupted as he retreated up the stairs, burning with embarrassment. Though it was his brother's outburst that had resulted in the shameful exit, it was ultimately caused by this corporal's actions.

And he had to pay.

Joachim headed into the bedchambers and toward the vanity in the corner his mother used for her makeup. But it wasn't her makeup he was interested in, it was the contents of one of the many drawers the handcrafted table contained. Months ago, he had spotted it, unbeknownst to her, when he had rushed into the room unannounced.

A small pistol.

A lady's pistol.

He had no idea what type it was. It wasn't anything he had been trained on as it wasn't military, and he had wondered why she had it, for it was certainly hers. His father wouldn't have such a dainty weapon.

Yet none of that mattered.

It was a weapon, it would have bullets, and he would use it to exact his revenge on the corporal who had embarrassed not only him, but his father, risking his entire family's future.

He pulled open the drawer, lipsticks and other things he didn't understand revealed.

But no gun.

His eyes narrowed.

Maybe it was a different drawer.

He shoved the drawer closed then pulled open a larger one, a smile spreading as he spotted the pistol grip underneath a large framed photo. He checked over his shoulder to confirm he was still alone, then retrieved the weapon. He examined it for a moment then ejected the magazine, confirming it was loaded.

He checked again to make sure nobody was looking, then smiled at the sight of his father's backup holster and Luger hanging on the wall. He drew a deep breath then stuffed his mother's weapon in his pocket, and was about to close the drawer when he noticed the photo. He picked it up, staring at it, his mind trying to place those it depicted. He recognized his parents among those gathered, though they appeared younger. But who were the others?

His eyes shot wide as a repressed memory escaped the dungeon he had forced it into long ago. He dropped the photo as if it were as hot as a cast iron pan, scrambling backward, tripping over a pair of his father's boots, his dagger sailing from his hand as he slammed into the floor.

It can't be!

Konrad Residence

Berlin, Nazi Germany

Maximilian's shoulders shook as he sobbed in his bed, his uniform still on, his pillow held tightly over his head. He had disappointed his father. He had embarrassed him on what was the most important night he could remember. Never before had he been witness to so many senior officers, so many women in dresses. Never before had he seen so many servants, so many fancy cars.

It had all been so exciting, something he had been looking forward to for days, his father putting so much trust in him to be on his best behavior.

And he had laughed.

It was wrong. He knew it. He should never have laughed at the corporal vomiting, but he couldn't' help it.

It was so funny!

He growled at his mattress in frustration. It was that corporal's fault.

I hate him!

A floorboard creaked in the hall and he froze, listening for any evidence as to who it was. It could be a servant, but it could be his mother, coming to see how he was doing after his admonishment, delivered by the *help* of all things.

Another creak, farther away, had his chest aching as it was obvious his mother wasn't coming to console him.

But who was it?

He rolled out of bed and opened the door slightly, his eyes widening at the sight of his brother slinking down the hallway toward the back stairs.

"Joachim! What are you doing?" he hissed.

His brother spun, his eyes wide with surprise, then glared at him angrily. He held a finger to his lips. "Go to bed," he whispered harshly.

Maximilian frowned but retreated back into his room, leaving the door open a sliver, his eye pressed against the crack that remained. His brother disappeared down the stairs.

Why does he get to rejoin the party?

He gently opened the door, then, spotting no one, sprinted toward the back stairs and after his brother. He descended the first flight then pressed against the window with a view of the corner of the house. The vomiting corporal was there, still on the side of the house where he had seen him earlier. He was about to resume his pursuit when his jaw dropped at the sight of his brother running along the rear of the house.

What's he doing outside?

His eyes bulged as Joachim drew a gun from his pocket.

Oh no!

Konrad Residence

Berlin, Nazi Germany

Griese continued his pacing, wearing a path in the grass between two large oak trees. His stomach continued to churn, though thankfully he had managed to control himself since the embarrassing incident several minutes ago. A servant had collected the children, and he hadn't seen anyone since, so he hoped they were the only ones to witness his terror.

For it was terror.

His mind was racing with every decision he had ever made that had brought him to this moment. From his earliest memories of running away from his first fight, to his decision to enlist at his parents' urging.

You must serve, boy!

He frowned.

Well, Father, are you happy now? Your boy is going to die because you wanted him to serve.

Someone sniffed behind him and his heart leaped into his throat as he spun toward the sound. It was Joachim, the eldest son, still in his Hitler Youth uniform, tears streaking his face, his nose runny.

Griese forgot his own troubles. "What's wrong, young man?"

"Y-you're what's wrong!" cried Joachim as he reached into his pocket, producing a small pistol. "It's all your fault!"

A wave of cowardice swept over him as he desperately wanted to run away, yet his legs refused to cooperate, and he instead felt faint. He raised his hands slowly, the only movement he could muster. "Be-be careful with that. You don't want to hurt anyone, now, do you?"

Joachim slowly circled him, the weapon now aimed directly at Griese's chest, though the arm holding it shook furiously. "You deserve to die for what you did!"

Griese backed away slowly then nearly cried out when he bumped into the wall of the house, his back pressed against the stone, his head against the sill. "What did I do?"

"You embarrassed me, and you embarrassed my father!"

The gun shook even more and Griese's eyes focused on the finger tucked into the trigger guard—it could go off accidentally at any moment. "Look, I'm not sure what you think I did, but why don't you put that gun down, and we'll go talk to your father."

The weapon steadied at the mention of the colonel.

"Or perhaps your mother? Perhaps we can talk to her, so your father doesn't need to know?"

He was grasping now. It was a small-caliber weapon, one he wasn't familiar with, but a lucky shot could kill him.

Thank God for small favors.

Death at the hands of this young boy might deliver him from his current predicament, though it would leave Joachim scarred for life. No sixteen-year-old should be forced to live with such a memory.

The weapon danced again at the mention of his mother, lowering slightly as a renewed eruption of tears flowed.

"My mother…"

Griese's eyes narrowed, and he lowered his voice. "What about your mother?"

"She…she…" He glared at him. "No! I can't tell you! No one can know!"

Griese's eyes widened as he realized what was happening.

The boy knew.

He knew the secret. He knew what Griese had discovered earlier in the evening, and had likely just discovered it himself.

He must not know what to think!

And that meant he was dangerous. His entire world was tearing apart, his indoctrination demanding he react in a way completely contrary to how a boy should when it came to his mother.

Empathize.

"I know her secret. Everything is going to be fine."

Joachim's eyes bulged. "Y-you know?"

"Yes, and it doesn't matter."

Joachim raised the weapon again and fired.

Konrad Residence

Berlin, Nazi Germany

A crack from outside was immediately followed by the shattering of glass, the large window behind Konrad's chair disintegrating. Someone screamed, Graf's companion, breaking the hushed silence that had fallen over the table, every woman at the table besides his wife erupting in panic.

She merely sat there and reached for her wine.

Konrad leaped to his feet, his chair tipping as the soldiers at the table rose in response, and though he was by no means the senior officer there, this was his house, and these were his guests.

They were all his responsibility. He pointed toward General Graf as his personal guard rushed into the room. "Protect the general! Get everyone to the shelter!"

"Yes, sir!"

He grabbed Renata and led her out of the room, pushing her into the crowd heading for the bomb shelter, then ran to the window to see if the assassin was still in the yard, though he suspected they were long gone, almost a minute having passed. Yet he was wrong. He spotted his corporal, Griese, standing near the remnants of the window.

"What have you done?"

Griese spun, staring up at him, blood running down his face, probably from a cut received when the glass collapsed from its frame. His eyes bulged, his jaw dropped, and he gulped several times, as if trying to find the words to explain the unexplainable.

"Guards, he's outside! Grab him!"

Konrad's head swiveled to see General Graf beside him, pointing at Griese. Heavy footfalls echoed through the hall as the orders were obeyed.

Griese bolted.

And Konrad cursed, one of his own who had already caused trouble tonight confirming his guilt.

He leaped through the open window to pursue when his wife screamed upstairs.

Palisaden Straße

Berlin, Nazi Germany

Griese sprinted into the darkness, his pulse pounding as the blood flowed from his ear and down the side of his face. He wiped at it with the back of his hand, but in the dark, it was merely a deeper shade of the gray that surrounded him. He heard footfalls to his left and was about to turn away when he realized it must be Joachim.

He turned left.

He had to catch the boy. His life depended on it. Right now, it was clear his commanding officer, and the terrifying SS general, believed he was the shooter. They had no reason to think otherwise. The shot had been fired, and he was the only one there moments later. Joachim had bolted immediately upon squeezing the trigger, and likely had no idea he had missed.

Mostly.

His ear was beginning to sting now, the adrenaline fueling those moments waning, the pain signals reaching his brain, no longer washed away by the stress of the situation.

He rounded a corner and skidded to a halt as the air raid sirens wailed around him. They were early tonight, perhaps a favorable tailwind bringing the Allied bombers here a little faster than usual. It might not bode well for them, as the sun had just set on the horizon, backlighting any bombers coming from that direction against the twilight sky.

The anti-aircraft fire pounded in the distance, the black smudges on the sky quickly blacking out any natural light, the harsh beams of the searchlights slicing through the chaos, crisscrossing the airspace in a bid to find targets for the gunners below.

The streets filled with civilians, rushing from their homes and toward their designated shelters, children wailing, mothers comforting, and fathers demanding everyone move faster.

He would never find Joachim in this cacophony of humanity.

He made his way through the crowds that were consolidating around the sandbagged entrances to the underground shelters, heading in the general direction he assumed Joachim would go—directly away from the house.

The boy was confused. He knew the secret kept from him, he knew the secret Griese had discovered earlier, a secret so stunning he had no idea how he would react if he were in Joachim's position.

Probably exactly as he is now.

The boy had tried to kill him, and had nearly succeeded, however he felt no malice toward the poor child. He simply wanted to find him and bring him back to his parents so he could explain what had happened. Perhaps together, with everyone aware of the secret the family had been hiding, he might escape the firing squad in his future should the course of this evening's events not change.

Someone darted into an alleyway to his right, away from the shelter, and he took a chance, running toward the shadow as the crowds rapidly dwindled, even the stragglers now in the shrinking lines to the shelters as the ground shook under his feet from the pounding of bombs in the distance.

A window shattered to his right and he spun toward the sound, then cursed as he spotted two men climbing into a now-empty house.

Looters.

The scum of society taking advantage of the war to enrich themselves. There was a rapidly growing black market in goods, and cash and items of value to trade were king. If he had the time, he'd shoot them both with his sidearm, but they weren't his concern.

"What are you looking at?"

He had been spotted. He opened his mouth to at least toss an admonishment their way, when he saw something move in the shadows, two more men emerging.

Get your ass out of here.

A gun was brandished and he sprinted after Joachim, laughter pursuing him rather than bullets. He arrived at the end of the alleyway and looked in both directions, seeing no one.

He could be anywhere.

He picked a direction, away from the residence, and continued at a slow jog, his head on a swivel. No one out now should be, and the boy still had the gun unless he had tossed it away during his flight from the scene.

Shouts behind him, in the distance, sounded more organized, more authoritative.

He tensed.

Were they after the looters?

Or were they after him, the man suspected in an assassination attempt only minutes ago.

No matter who they were, it wouldn't do him any good to be found roaming the streets, away from his post, with no explanation beyond a futile search for the real shooter.

He shuddered from the evening chill and his predicament.

At this very moment, every single person he might encounter had reason to harm him.

Or worse.

Konrad Residence

Berlin, Nazi Germany

"Why aren't you downstairs with the others?"

Konrad's wife spun toward him, her face pale, her hands trembling. Her eyes darted toward her vanity and he spotted the open drawer, a forbidden photo visible. His heart leaped into his throat and he turned, holding out his arms as two of his staff rushed into the room, responding to her cry.

"Everybody out!" He ushered them back into the hallway then pointed to the stairs. "Secure the grounds, and make certain my guests are safe in the shelter." They both snapped to attention then sprinted down the hallway. "And report the incident! We need to find Corporal Griese!"

"Yes, sir!"

He retreated to the bedroom, locking the outer door behind him, then headed quickly to the inner chambers, his wife now sitting on the edge of the bed.

"What's going on? Quickly now, we don't have much time before more arrive."

She pointed at the drawer. "It's gone."

A lump forced its way up his throat and he rushed to the desk, everything appearing in order, though what was currently visible could pose trouble should it be seen by the wrong people.

"Was it open like this when you came in here?"

She nodded.

"What's missing? Everything looks in order to me."

"My pistol."

His eyes narrowed. "Your pistol?" He paused, not certain as to what she was speaking of. Then he remembered. "Oh. I had forgotten about that. You kept it here?"

"Yes."

He rifled through the drawer, not finding it. "You're sure you kept it in *this* drawer?"

"Yes."

The air raid sirens tore through the calm of the capital and he rushed to the balcony, cursing at the sight in the distance, his beloved city once again under bombardment from planes the Luftwaffe had promised could never reach here. He clasped his hands behind his back, staring as the battle raged in the distance, explosions tearing into the night sky as the Allied bombs found their marks.

"Rudy!"

He snapped out of his soldier persona, returning to that of husband. He stepped inside and shut the doors to the balcony, drawing closed the blackout drapes. Something occurred to him and he turned to his wife.

"Why did you come up here?"

She clasped her hands in front of her. "I recognized the sound."

"What?"

"The gunshot. I recognized it from when I practiced shooting."

He smiled slightly, impressed. "You never cease to amaze me. It hadn't even occurred to me, but you're right." He scratched his chin. "Why would Griese use a weapon like that?" He sat beside her. "And why would he come and get yours?" His eyes narrowed. "In fact, how would he ever have known it was there?"

Renata sighed deeply, her shoulders sagging. "There is a way, but it wasn't him."

Konrad put his arm over her shoulders. "What do you mean? Who was it?"

She pointed to their left and he turned his head and gasped.

It was Joachim's Hitler Youth dagger, lying on the floor.

"Oh no!" He jumped to his feet, rushing toward it then snatched it. There was no doubt what it was, the insignia unmistakable, and there would only be one in the house—Maximilian was too young to have been issued a dagger as he was still classified as a 'youngster' in the organization. He turned slowly toward his wife, the implications still a disorganized mess of thoughts. Griese had been at the window, he hadn't had a weapon in his hand, despite wearing his sidearm, and he had been bleeding.

Could he have been shot?

Could he have been shot by Joachim?

He refused to believe it.

He charged from the room and out into the hallway, his feet pounding on the floor as he headed for Joachim's room. He tore open the door and switched on the light, then cursed at the empty bed.

"Joachim!"

"He went outside."

He spun to see Maximilian, peering out from behind the door of his room. "What?"

"He went outside. I think he had a gun." Maximilian rushed from the room and hugged his father's legs. "Father, what's going on?"

Konrad wasn't certain, but he couldn't let his son know that. "Nothing that concerns you. And why aren't you in the shelter? Can't you hear the sirens?"

"You're not there."

Konrad gave his son a look and pointed toward the stairs. "To the shelter. Now."

Maximilian let go of Konrad's legs then headed down the hall, Konrad watching after him as his worst fears had been confirmed. His son had fired the shot, and he had fired it at Griese. But why? And did anyone else know?

He stared at the retreating figure of his son and tensed.

"Maximilian?"

His son turned. "Yes, Father?"

"If anyone asks, you never saw your brother. Understood?"

"You want me to lie?"

"I want you to protect your brother, and the Reich."

Maximilian sucked in a quick breath at the mention of the Reich, his shoulders squaring. "Yes, sir!"

Konrad flicked his wrist toward the stairs. "To the shelter."

"Yes, Father."

He disappeared around the corner, his tiny footfalls echoing down the stairs, and Konrad returned to his bedchambers, his wife pacing in front of the bed.

"Joachim?"

"Gone. Maximilian says he saw him leave with the gun."

She collapsed onto the bed, wrapping her arms around her chest. "What are we going to do?"

"We have to find him and Griese before they do."

She paled. "There's something you need to know about Griese."

Her tone had his entire body taut. "What?"

"I think he knows."

Strausberger Straße

Berlin, Nazi Germany

Griese flinched then froze, tilting his head slightly and cocking an ear. He had heard something. He was certain of it. Yet was he? The Allied bombers were hammering the western outskirts of the city, and between the Luftwaffe's response and the air defenses firing at anything with the misfortune of having been caught in the searchlights, he could be forgiven for being uncertain.

His heart was pounding now, and he committed, turning around and peering into the darkness. It was partially overcast, though perhaps it was smoke from the fires now burning in the west rather than clouds, and the moon was a quarter at best. The city was blacked out, the streetlights dark, and the citizenry hidden away in public or private bomb shelters.

No one should be on the street.

Though he was, and shouldn't be.

He needed time to think. Too much was happening all at once. He had seen something he should never have seen. He had humiliated an SS general. He had embarrassed his commanding officer. He had been shot at by his commanding officer's eldest son, who also had seen what he shouldn't.

It was all too much, though there might be a way out of it.

He had seen something he shouldn't have seen, and that knowledge gave him leverage, should he be willing to use it.

Yet he couldn't.

Could he? Right now, he was certain he was marked for death. He had technically left his post, disobeyed an order, and was likely about to be reassigned to the Eastern Front if not featuring prominently in the next line of executions.

His duty as a soldier of the Third Reich was clear. He should report what he had seen to his superior. But his superior officer was involved, so that was out of the question. He could report it outside of his chain of command, though that would mean the certain death of at least one innocent person, perhaps more.

Is your life worth any more than theirs?

He sighed, his shoulders slumping, deciding to abandon his search for the boy and return to the colonel's residence to face what was to come.

Though he wasn't in a hurry to do so.

The bombers never reached this part of the city, content to deliver their payload over the primary targets to the west, every drop of fuel precious at these ranges. There was a better chance of being hit by a car driving without lights than a stray bomb.

Though none of that mattered.

He was dead regardless if he didn't report what he had seen. Konrad couldn't risk him knowing. If Mrs. Konrad had seen him, and had told her husband, then they would act quickly, perhaps even tonight. He paused in mid-step, one foot in front of him hovering.

Why are you going back there?

If he returned, he was walking directly into the wolf's lair. It was insanity to do so. He should be going to Headquarters, not back to the scene of the crime.

For it was a crime, and as a German citizen, a German soldier, even a lowly corporal, he had to report it. His duty to the state had been drummed into him since he was a child in the Hitler Youth.

Duty before all else, even family.

And this was self-preservation. If nobody knew he had discovered their secret, then perhaps he could sit back and remain silent, allowing someone else to inevitably discover the truth. But Joachim now knew the secret, and also knew *he* knew. Once Joachim was found, or returned home of his own volition, the truth would come out, and they'd be forced to act.

Something that would be too easy if he were sitting in his quarters or standing at his post.

You have to report it. It's not your place to choose which orders to obey.

He frowned. Reporting it could be used as an excuse for leaving his post, and for why he had disobeyed the last order given to him. It could save him from a court-martial. He could even use the freshness of the discovery as an excuse for the events that had caused so much embarrassment earlier.

Everything could be excused.

It could save his life.

You did nothing wrong. Why should you pay?

A decision was made, one he wasn't sure he'd be happy with tomorrow, but one he could see no alternative to. He drew a breath then blew it out heavily. He regained his bearings and turned to his right, toward Headquarters.

Then stopped.

You can't do this. It's not right.

A shoe scraped behind him.

Approaching the Konrad Residence

Berlin, Nazi Germany

Konrad walked briskly toward his new home, his pistol drawn and at his side, his entire body tense with the events of the evening. What was to have been a pleasant dinner party to fulfill the expectations of his position, had turned into a nightmare. His son was missing, though more importantly, his son had discovered the family secret and had obviously not reacted well.

Can you blame him?

The boy's entire world was collapsing around him, and he wouldn't know who to trust, or where to go. And with the dozen empty troop carriers lined up in front of his house, SS swarming the area and breaking off into search parties, the danger to his son and the rest of the family grew with every moment.

If he tells them…

He shuddered at the thought.

If he tells them, we're all finished.

"Rudy!"

He turned to see his wife emerge from the shadows and his eyes widened. "What are you doing out?"

"I had to go look. He's my son."

Konrad's chest ached at the pain in her voice. He was her son, and she would love him no matter what, even if he hated her, and likely wanted her dead.

It was a situation no family should be in.

She looked about at the frenzy of activity. "Have they found him?"

Konrad took her by the hand and led her back onto the grounds. "No, I don't believe so. But we will."

"And Griese?"

His heart sprinted at the mention of the name. "They'll find him."

As they climbed the stairs to their home, the all-clear sounded, and he pointed toward the bedrooms. "Go to our room. I'll see our guests out."

"Yes, my love." She hurried up the stairs as the first of their visitors emerged from the basement, the cars already idling outside, the chauffeurs ready to ferry their VIPs home to check on the state of their own appropriated abodes.

Regrets were exchanged, everyone understanding except the last to depart, General Graf.

"Not a smooth evening, Colonel."

Konrad bowed his head slightly. "It had its unfortunate moments."

"An attempt on one of your guest's lives is hardly an 'unfortunate moment.'"

Konrad flushed. "A poor attempt at humor, sir."

"Indeed." Graf eyed him for a moment. "I wonder, Colonel, if we made a mistake with you."

Konrad's cheeks drained of any blood they might have had. "I can assure you, sir, you haven't. We will apprehend the perpetrator, and bring him to justice."

Graf stared at him, his eyes boring deep into Konrad's psyche, a tremble threatening to erupt. "You have twenty-four hours, then I take over."

"Yes, sir."

"And I expect a full report in the morning."

"You'll have it."

Graf turned on his heel and headed down the stairs and out of sight, leaving Konrad a shaking mess.

Konrad Residence

Berlin, Nazi Germany

"I can't believe you were so stupid!"

Renata wept on the side of the bed, a handkerchief pressed into the corners of her eyes as she sobbed, her shoulders heaving with each gasp as Konrad lay into her, pacing back and forth, shouting at the ceiling, paying little attention to her.

For he wasn't mad at her.

He was terrified for her, and their children.

"How could you keep that photo? How could you let our son see that?"

"I-I'm sorry." She lay down on the bed, curling into a ball. "I can't take this anymore. The lying. The constant fear. I'm finished with it."

He froze, turning toward her, finally paying attention to her anguish. His stomach flipped as his tirade at her expense replayed itself, and he felt nauseous. He sat beside her and put a hand on her shoulder. "I'm sorry. I shouldn't have yelled at you. I'm just…" He sighed. "I'm just scared."

"You don't think I am?"

He draped himself over her, holding her tight as he squeezed his eyes shut. "I know, dear, I know. But we'll get through this if we remain calm. If we act differently, people will start to ask questions."

She sniffed loudly then sat up. She wiped her eyes then blew her nose before looking at him. "What are we going to do?"

He pointed at the drawer containing the photo. "You're going to burn that, and anything else you've been keeping."

"Not…"

He knew what she was speaking of, and he understood her reluctance. He sighed. "No, I suppose not. But you must be more careful. Lock the door."

"What are we going to do about Griese?"

"Griese is dead."

Her eyes widened. "Really? Do-do you know who killed him?"

He rose, waving a hand at her. "No, I mean, General Graf thinks he tried to kill one of our guests tonight. He'll be executed as soon as they find him. As long as he says nothing, then the secret is safe."

She frowned, staring at the handkerchief she gripped. "But what of Joachim?"

He sighed. "We must find him. Explain to him what's going on, and why he must remain quiet. He'll come around eventually."

"He's a good boy, but I fear his loyalty is to Hitler and not his family."

He stared at the heavily draped window. "You might be right. Let's just hope that whoever finds him first, simply brings him home instead of asking him questions."

"Questions will get everyone killed."

He sighed. "I think we have to plan for the worst."

She stared at him. "What's there to plan for? What to wear to our funerals?"

He smiled slightly, taking her hands as he struggled to maintain the brave face. "No, I mean we should go into hiding."

Renata's eyes widened and she leaned back in her chair, freeing her hands. "Are you serious?"

"It's preferable to death, isn't it?"

She folded her arms, looking about the room. "Well, yes, of course, but I mean, it's a ridiculous notion, isn't it? Where would we go?"

"I was thinking my sister's."

"Wouldn't that be one of the first places they'd look? Surely they'll go to our relatives first."

"Yes, at first. But if we hide in the forest for a couple of weeks, they'll give up searching for us."

"The forest? You're mad." She shook her head. "I just can't see how it would work. And besides, I'm not going anywhere until we find Joachim, and you said we only have, what, twenty-four hours?"

He checked his watch to reconfirm what he already knew. "Yes, before he starts his investigation. But it will take time before they discover our secret. Perhaps days, even weeks, though they will find it."

"But I thought you destroyed all the records?"

"I destroyed or altered what I could, but there are certainly copies out there somewhere. And the absence of records raises suspicions as well. By destroying them, I might have created a situation where proof of our innocence is demanded, and if we can't produce it, we'll be found guilty regardless."

She closed her eyes, her shoulders sagging. "I don't know what to do. There has to be a better way."

He rose, pacing once again as he clasped his hands behind his back. "What that might be, I have no idea. We can't just sit here and wait to die."

"Find Griese. That's the only option."

"But how? I've got hundreds of troops out searching the city. Every post has been notified to be on the lookout for him. Roadblocks are being set up. I don't know what else I can do."

She sighed heavily. "That's useless. All of it. He's probably changed into civilian clothes by now, and nobody knows what he looks like unless you've made copies of his photo and distributed them everywhere."

"That's underway, but it takes time."

"Exactly. He'll have lost himself in the city. The only way you'll ever find him is if it's by pure accident."

He regarded her for a moment. "You're not helping."

She shrugged. "I'm just telling you the truth."

He groaned, staring at the ceiling. "I know, I know." He laughed. "It's too bad the general saw him. We could just pick out anybody, put him in a uniform, and say that's him."

She paused. "That's not such a terrible idea."

His eyebrows shot up. "Excuse me? You do know that Griese will be executed, whether it's actually him or not."

She smiled. "What if he were already dead?"

Strausberger Straße

Berlin, Nazi Germany

"Look at this poor bastard."

Carl Vetter shook his head at the sight. A young man, dead, lying under some garbage in an alleyway. Naked. He motioned toward the man's exposed private parts. "At least cover him back up, Fritz. Let the poor guy have some dignity."

Fritz grunted. "I don't think he much cares now, does he?"

"If it were you, would you want your bratwurst on display?"

Fritz frowned. "I guess not." He picked up one of the pieces of cardboard moved only moments ago, and strategically placed it over the man's groin. He stepped back and pointed. "There's blood underneath him."

"Shot in the back?"

"Probably looters. Wouldn't be the first time."

"Well, somebody's going to miss him. I'll call the *Orpo*. Let the police decide what to do with him."

Fritz frowned. "Why not just cover him back up and let someone else deal with it. We're going to be here all night if we get involved."

Vetter shook his head. "You're pathetic." He jabbed a finger at the body. "What if it were you? Would you want to just be left there for hours, or days? Soon the vermin will be getting at him. Would you want your mother to see you like that, all torn apart?" He sighed heavily. "Sometimes I wonder about you."

Fritz shrugged. "So, I'm a prince. What can you do?" He pointed at the man's head. "Looks like the rats have already been gnawing on him. Check out his ear."

Vetter frowned, finally noticing evidence of bites all over the body. "I'm going to make the call. The sooner this poor soul is off the street the better." He stared toward the street as another troop transport drove by. "And I want to get out of here. There's an awful lot of SS out tonight for some reason. Whatever's going on, I don't want to be mixed up in it."

"Yet another reason to just cover him back up."

Vetter chewed his cheek, rethinking things. Fritz might be right on this one. Troop transports had been rolling past since they arrived here after the air raid all-clear was sounded. It was late, most good people were home, and he was one of those assigned to assess bomb damage and take reports of any thefts. If the SS had an interest in this area, it wasn't related to the air raid, as none of the bombs had reached this end of the city.

Something was going on, and it couldn't be good.

He stared at the young man lying on the ground, then checked each end of the alley, seeing no one.

"Cover him up. Let's get the hell out of here."

Vogel Residence

Berlin, Nazi Germany

"Thank God that's over," sighed Sofia Vogel as she stepped through the door to their apartment. "I don't think I'll ever get used to that."

Kriminalinspektor Wolfgang Vogel closed the door behind them, relieving himself of his hat and jacket as his wife doublechecked that the windows were covered before he turned the light on. "I'm afraid you might have to. It's only going to get worse."

"Nonsense. Once we take England, they'll have nowhere to fly from." Her voice changed in the pitch black as she turned toward him. "We're good."

He turned on the light in the entryway and blinked several times, adjusting to the abrupt change. He pulled off his shoes then wiggled his toes before entering the living room and dropping into his chair. "I don't think the British will make it that easy for us."

His wife headed for the kitchen, the sounds of tea being prepared comforting in its normalcy after the stress of an air raid. He leaned back and put his feet up on the table, his eyes closing as he slowly relaxed.

"Feet off the table."

He smiled, removing them. "How'd you know?"

"I know you."

He chuckled. "When are the kids due back?"

"Tomorrow morning. Thank God they missed the raid. They would have been terrified."

He frowned. "They'll have to get used to it too."

She poked her head out of the kitchen. "You really think so?"

He turned in his chair. "Absolutely. Things will get worse before they get better."

She returned to the kitchen. "But they *will* get better, right?"

I hope so.

"I'm sure they will."

"Well, if you're not worried, then I won't worry." She emerged with a tea service, placing it on the table where his feet had been perched. She waved him off from pouring. "You relax. You've had a long day, and you'll be back at it in the morning."

He smiled at her. "You're too good to me."

She handed him his cup. "And don't you forget it."

He took a sip and sighed, relaxing his head against the back of his chair, the tension easing from his body. "Hopefully this damned war will be over soon, and life can get back to normal."

His wife sat in her chair on the opposite side of the small table that separated them, lowering her voice. "Sometimes I wonder why we had to go to war in the first place. Things were going so well."

He grunted. "Be careful who you say stuff like that in front of. You're liable to find yourself at Gestapo headquarters."

She smiled. "You'll save me."

He shook his head. "Even I can't save you from them." He glanced toward the door, his eyes fixating on the Nazi Party pin on his jacket. It symbolized his loyalty to the Party, to the state, to the Führer Adolf Hitler.

And represented nothing he stood for.

He was a police officer. A detective. His job was to solve crimes, mostly homicides. He had been on the force before the Nazis came to power, and when the new regime had forced everyone to join the Party and swear an oath of allegiance to Hitler to keep their jobs, he had gone along with it out of necessity.

There were many on the force, too many, that had bought into the propaganda and believed wholeheartedly in the war and the policies of the Nazis. He didn't blame them. Things had been hell in Germany after the *Weltkrieg*, the World War, and the punitive measures contained within the Treaty of Versailles. Life was far better now. Far. But if the war didn't go well, as these things tended to do, things could return to the horrid conditions of only a decade ago.

Yet it wasn't their fierce loyalty to the Führer that offended him. People were entitled to their own beliefs.

On their own time.

A police officer should be above politics, above ideologies. He should be devoted to law and order, to serving the public, to protecting the innocent. Unfortunately, too often, he witnessed fellow officers reporting every little thing they saw to the SS or Gestapo, using their positions of authority to seek petty vengeance on anyone that upset them in any way.

It was sickening.

And unfortunately for him, his partner, Otto Stadler, was one of them. He was young, had spent much of his childhood in the Hitler Youth, and had been fully taken in by the Nazi ideology. When he had been assigned to Vogel last year, it had been a horrible day. His old partner, a man he had worked with most of his career, had retired early, leaving the country before the war began, a postcard that arrived a few months later the only word Vogel had received from him.

All it said was, "Wish you were here!" and the man's initials.

The other side was the Statue of Liberty, an American stamp and postmark proving its origins.

He had known what was coming, and escaped while he had the chance.

Much easier when you were a committed bachelor and didn't have a wife and two young children.

Now Vogel had to be extremely careful about what he said and did around Stadler. The kid was slowly softening. Not in his ideals or beliefs, but in the way he handled himself. He had finally begun to realize that the law was not absolute. It was bendable. Just because someone broke the letter of the law, didn't mean they had to be reported. People were people. They made mistakes.

And besides, they were *Kripo*, Kriminalpolizei, Criminal Police. Specifically, they were homicide detectives. They weren't supposed to be cracking down on people committing a traffic infraction or stealing a loaf of bread. Leave that to the uniformed officers, the Orpo. The Kripo were there to investigate the worst of what humanity was capable of. And despite the war, the depraved still lurked in the shadows, committing their ghastly deeds.

It kept him busy, though it was something he would gladly give up if it meant no more murder.

Though the likelihood of that was nil.

Something slipped under the front door and he jumped to his feet, putting his cup down and rushing toward the entrance. He ignored the piece of paper and instead yanked open the door to see a figure at the far end of the hall, entering the stairwell. He couldn't make out his face in the dark, the lights in the common areas removed due to the war effort.

But he was pretty certain it was one of his neighbors from downstairs, Carl Vetter.

He obviously didn't want you to know it was him.

He stepped back inside and closed the door. He picked up the folded piece of paper and read it, frowning.

There's a body in the alleyway between the baker and post office on Strausberger Street.

He tilted his head back, imagining exactly where that was, then checked his watch. He groaned. It never ended.

"Another neighbor complaining about somebody again?"

He grunted. "I wish. I'm pretty sure it was Carl from downstairs. He says there's a body near Strausberger Street."

His wife regarded him. "What does that have to do with you?"

"Umm, I'm a *homicide* detective?"

"Exactly. *Homicide.* This could be someone killed in the bombing for all you know."

He wagged a finger at her as he picked up the receiver on the home phone, usually reserved for official duties. "You're forgetting who the messenger is."

"Carl. So?"

"So, he works with the *Reichsluftschutzbund,* the Air Raid Protection League. If the body were related to the air raid, then it would be his job to deal with it."

She leaned back in her chair, her argument defeated. "Then he thinks it's murder."

"Hey, Otto, it's me. I just got a tip that there's a body at Strausberger Street, between the bakery and the post office. I'm leaving now. Meet you there?"

"Yes, sir!"

Vogel shook his head as he hung up. "I think that kid just clicked his heels in bed."

Sofia snickered. "He is rather eager, isn't he?"

"Too much. I never felt old until I met him."

"Old? You're nowhere near forty!"

He held his arms out and she rose to embrace him. "I'm closer to it than you are. What are you, twenty-three, twenty-four?"

She laughed, swatting him on the chest. "You wish!"

He grinned then leaned over and gave her a peck. "You're more beautiful every day."

She squeezed his chin. "And you're more handsome every day too." She winked. "Especially in the dark."

He swatted her behind then let her go and headed for the door. He donned his trench coat and hat, then shoved his sidearm in its holster. "Don't wait up, and don't worry if you don't see me until tomorrow night. If this is a homicide, I'll be busy. I'll try to call in the morning to let you know either way."

She straightened his collar then popped up on her toes to give him a quick kiss. "Be careful."

"I always am."

He stepped into the hall then blew her a kiss through the sliver of doorway visible, then headed for the stairwell, his footsteps echoing through the hall. He drew a deep breath, closing his eyes for a moment, the lids burning from fatigue. He was exhausted and needed sleep.

Desperately.

Let's just hope this is a nice, easy case.

Konrad Residence

Berlin, Nazi Germany

"It's done."

Renata rose from her chair and held out her hands, taking Konrad's in hers. "You look horrible."

He sighed, dropping into his chair, his wife returning to hers. "You would too if you'd just been dealing with the dead."

Renata poured him some tea and he took the cup. "Well? Did you find, umm, him?"

Konrad frowned then took a sip. "Yes, I found *him*."

She sighed. "Then that's at least one less thing to have to worry about." She paused. "Two, I guess. Have you told the general yet?"

He shook his head. "No, we have to let the system find him." He sniffed. "Ugh, I smell like death."

She turned up her nose slightly. "I didn't want to say anything." She pointed at his uniform. "I'll have it cleaned for you. Unless you want it burned?"

He chuckled. "Is it that bad?"

"It grows worse with every moment I'm in the room with it." She pointed at his chest. "And there's, umm, something on it."

He cringed at the sight and set his tea down. "I'll take care of it." He rose then paused. "Joachim?"

Gloom clouded her face. "Still no word. I'm really worried."

"As am I. I hope they find *him* soon. As long as Griese is still missing, those troops are out there looking for him *and* our son."

"I just don't know where he'd go. It's been so long. He must be tired and cold. And he probably hasn't eaten since lunch."

He patted her on her shoulder. "He's your son. He's strong. He can take care of himself. Rest assured, I will find him, even if I have to pound on every door in this city personally."

Strausberger Straße

Berlin, Nazi Germany

Kriminalinspektor Wolfgang Vogel shone his flashlight over the pile of garbage covering the naked body found exactly where Vetter's note had said it would be. The streets were empty of civilians, the SS swarming the area for some reason, and despite the fact he was SS on the organizational chart, he didn't bother asking what they were up to.

They might be looking for this poor bastard.

If they were, then they'd take possession of the body and he'd be left with no hope of solving the case. Though there wasn't much of a case, if his initial impression was correct. A naked body, found tossed in an alleyway, covered over, after an air raid. He'd seen it before, and he'd see it again. This poor soul probably tried to stop looters from robbing his home, or that of his neighbors, and paid the ultimate price for being a good Samaritan.

I hate thieves.

As far as he was concerned, people who stole should be shot, not imprisoned. They took from those who worked hard, as if they were entitled to it. When caught, the claims that they stole to survive were sometimes believable, yet were still no excuse. There were charities that could help, and Germany was a much different place now. If one was truly desperate, then join the Army and fight for one's country. Steady pay, food, clothing, shelter. What more could one want? Yes, one could die in battle, but the same was true on the streets, and perhaps as likely.

Especially once they started shooting looters.

They hadn't really started yet, though with the problem growing with each air raid, those that would leech off society were surging in number and emboldened with each success. The citizens wouldn't put up with it much longer, and the Party would deal with it as it made them look bad—the Fatherland was supposed to be left untouched.

Reichsmarschall Hermann Göring had promised no Allied bombers would reach the Fatherland.

Well, you got that wrong, Meyer.

"What have we got?"

Vogel turned to see his partner, Otto Stadler, approaching, his own flashlight lighting his way. "Dead body. I haven't started yet." He put his flashlight away and bent down, Stadler's light casting a dull glow for him to work by. He gently removed the scrap cardboard and wood covering the body, confirming the victim was indeed naked. "Looks young. Mid to late teens, perhaps early twenties. Hard to tell in this light."

"Baby-faced."

Vogel agreed. It was a good way to describe the man—boy. He examined him for wounds, finding his body covered in dozens of tiny bite marks. "He's been here long enough for the rats to start making a meal out of him."

"Disgusting. When we're done with the British and the Russians, we should focus the Wehrmacht's efforts on those vermin."

Vogel chuckled. "Good idea. Why don't you send a memo to Himmler? It might become the next great cause."

"Sometimes I can't tell if your jokes are meant to belittle me or the regime."

Vogel rolled his eyes, out of sight of his partner. This was the problem with Stadler. He always had to be so careful with what he said around him. "I assure you, it was entirely at your expense."

Stadler grunted. "I still think it's a good idea."

"I don't see anything that would kill him on the front of his body, but there's a pool of blood here. I'm going to flip him." He gently lifted the left side of the body, making sure there was no wound where he was about to gain leverage, then finding nothing beyond the filth of the ground, pushed him over onto his stomach.

Revealing a gunshot wound to the center of the back.

"Well, that would do it."

Stadler knelt beside him, shining the light on the wound. "Looks close range."

Vogel nodded. He took out his own flashlight and leaned in, his eyes mere centimeters from the body. "There's some material in the wound.

We'll have the guys in the lab look at it. Maybe they can identify what he was wearing."

"What good will that do? He was wearing a shirt and coat. Everyone has a shirt and coat."

Vogel rose. "You have so much to learn. What kind of material was it? What color? What if it was a uniform he was wearing? What if it was a leather jacket and we find one discarded around here with a hole in the back? There's so much we could learn by getting those fibers under a microscope."

Stadler chewed his lip. "I suppose."

Vogel gestured toward the street with his chin. "Call it in. I want the body in the morgue so the coroner's medical examiner can take a look at him."

"Right away." Stadler turned when Vogel reached out and grabbed his arm. "And get some uniformed officers down here. I want this area searched just in case his clothes were tossed somewhere. Maybe a wallet with some ID. And we're going to have to canvas all the residences around here. Somebody might have heard something."

"During an air raid? Everyone was in the shelters."

Vogel shook his head, disappointed. "You think in such black and white terms. Just because the law says they have to seek shelter, doesn't mean they do. Everyone knows by now the Allies can't reach this section of the city. I'm willing to bet half these people just stayed home, waiting for the bombs to get close enough to worry about."

"You think so many of our good citizens would disobey the law like that? You think so little of your country?"

"Son, if everyone obeyed the law like you think they should, then this man wouldn't be dead, and we wouldn't have jobs. People break laws. That's why we have police. Even in Adolf Hitler's Germany."

Stadler bristled, unhappy with the lecture. His shoulders relaxed. "I suppose you're right. It disgusts me, but I suppose you're right."

Vogel pointed toward the street where his car was. "Call it in."

Stadler thrust his chest out and snapped his heels. "Yes, sir!"

Konrad Residence

Berlin, Nazi Germany

"What's going on?"

Maximilian's face broke out into a smile at the voice of his friend. He rolled to the edge of the bed, pressing his ear against the wall. "Frida, is that you?"

"Of course it is. You were expecting someone else?"

He giggled. "No, I suppose not. You haven't heard?"

"No, what?"

"Joachim is missing. I think he ran away."

"Why would he do that?"

Maximilian wasn't sure how much he should reveal to his secret friend, despite the fact she was the only person he trusted in the entire world. She never lied to him. She never got angry with him. She was his friend. His best friend.

His only friend.

His brother treated him horribly, his father didn't have time for him, and his mother barely spoke to anyone for as long as he could remember. This house was so unhappy, it made him cry all the time.

He hated it here.

He hated his family.

A pit formed in his stomach at the thought. He didn't understand what was going on around him. He realized that. He was too young. Joachim understood, or at least understood better than him. But he was sixteen. He'd be leaving soon, then he'd be an officer.

Maximilian drew a breath, eager to have the house to himself. And in two years he'd be twelve, almost a teenager.

"Max? Are you there?"

He pressed harder against the wall. "Yes. Sorry. Umm, I don't know why, but I think he had a gun."

"A gun! Where'd he get that?"

"I don't know. I think my parents' room, but I can't be certain."

"That's scary. Did you tell them what you saw?"

His father's words came back to him and his chest tightened as he realized he had broken his word. "Umm, I shouldn't say."

"Come on, Max, it's me. You know I can't tell anyone."

Can't.

He sighed at the choice of words. He had told his brother about Frida when he had first heard her voice, and he had laughed at him, teasing him relentlessly about his imaginary friend. He had run crying to his mother, who had consoled him and told him that she too had an imaginary friend when she was his age.

"They're the best friends you can have when you're feeling lonely. They're always there when you need them, you can tell them anything and they'll never tell on you, and when you no longer need them, they just go away, and no one's feelings are hurt."

You can tell them anything.

He smiled. It meant he had his mother's blessing. "I told my father. He seemed, I don't know, concerned? He told me to tell no one what I saw."

"But you told me. Thanks, Max, that means a lot."

He smiled. "Did you hear the air raid?"

"Yes. It was so scary."

"I wasn't scared."

"Yes you were!"

He giggled. "You're right, I guess I was. It's too bad it happened tonight. My father had a bunch of officers here for dinner. It ruined the party."

"I'm glad they're gone."

His eyes narrowed. "Why?"

"I get scared when there are people in the house."

His eyes widened. "Why? I love it when there are people here. Otherwise it's so boring."

The door to the room burst open and his father stood silhouetted by the hallway light. "Who are you talking to? Is Joachim in here?" He flipped the light switch and quickly searched the room as Maximilian pressed his back against the wall, his legs drawn up to his chest, gripping his blanket, his eyes wide with fear.

"Who are you talking to!"

"No-nobody."

"I heard you talking."

"I-I was talking to myself." Tears erupted and his father glared at him, making it even worse. He squeezed his eyes shut, burying his head under the blanket. "I'm sorry, Father, I won't do it again."

The bed moved as his father sat on it, and he flinched as arms embraced him, holding him tight. "It's all right. I'm sorry for yelling at you. I'm just so worried about your brother."

Maximilian extricated himself from the blanket then wrapped his arms around his father's neck. "Is he dead?"

His father's breath caught for a moment, and he knew that was exactly what his father was thinking. "No, I'm sure he's fine. He's just out there, scared. We'll find him." His father pushed him away gently, and wiped the tears from Maximilian's cheeks. "Now, you get some sleep. It's late, and I'm sure tomorrow will be busy."

"Yes, Father."

His father rose and turned out the light. "And no more talking to imaginary friends."

Maximilian's eyes widened. "How'd you know?"

"Your mother tells me everything." His father smiled. "And I had one too when I was your age. What's his name?"

"It's a she."

The smile faded slightly. "Very well, what's *her* name?"

"Frida."

"I see."

He closed the door without saying anything else, leaving Maximilian with the distinct impression he wasn't happy about something.

Strausberger Straße

Berlin, Nazi Germany

"What the hell is this?"

Vogel sighed. They had been waiting for hours for the coroner's office to send a vehicle to pick up their victim, and they had so far managed to avoid any interaction with the SS rushing about. But with the vehicle finally arriving, they had become a spectacle, and from the arrogance in the voice, whoever was behind him was likely one of those they had successfully sidestepped until now.

He would need to tread lightly.

He turned, smiling at the young junior officer whom he barely outranked in the command structure, despite being almost twice his age. "A murder victim. Probably looters." He waved at the SS still searching the area. "What are you looking for?"

"That's none of your concern!"

Vogel's smile climbed up one side of his cheek. "Of course it isn't, but if the Kriminalpolizei can be of any assistance, just ask."

"And you are?"

"Kriminalinspektor Vogel."

The man's eyes flared slightly and his entire demeanor changed as he realized he was outranked. "I apologize for interrupting you, Kriminalinspektor. Can *we* be of any assistance?"

Vogel shook his head. "No." He decided the terse answer was the best, leaving no wiggle room for the lieutenant.

"Very well." A salute and heel click were delivered, then the lieutenant rushed off with his men.

"Well, that was idiotic."

Vogel turned to Stadler as the truck was closed up, their body inside. "You mean that he didn't bother to look to see if we had who he was looking for in the back?"

"Exactly."

"See what happens when you think in such black and white terms? It would never occur to him that our lowly duties could ever intersect with his orders. He's looking for someone of such importance in his mind, he couldn't possibly fathom that they could be a victim of such a petty thing as looting."

Stadler frowned as the coroner's wagon pulled away. "I suppose so. He's young. He'll learn."

Vogel suppressed a smile. Stadler was lucky to be a year older than the young lieutenant.

Though the war has them all growing up quicker than they should.

He prayed the war would be over before his children were of age. Hopefully, with Germany victorious, things would relax and the strict code they were forced to live under might ease up slightly as things returned to normal.

But what was normal? He had been a child during the World War, during which life was tough. Then the retribution exacted by the victors in the form of the Treaty of Versailles had made the Great Depression far worse for Germany than anywhere else in the world. He, like most, had grown up poor, hungry, and angry. Then Hitler had arrived, at first thought of as a madman, he had swiftly gained popularity, then seized power.

Somewhat democratically.

And things had improved. Dramatically. Drastically. The only truly good times he knew were under the Nazis. How life was before the first war was something he could barely remember, and children rarely knew how rough things actually were—their parents protected them from the truth as much as possible.

He had been lucky. An uncle was on the force and had got him a job, years before the Nazis took power. It had been the proudest moment of his life. Second most. His proudest was the day he married his beloved Sofia. He smiled slightly. Fourth most? The birth of his children had to rank up there somewhere.

Proudest professional moment.

That was absolutely true. It meant an honorable profession, a steady income, and every year he remained meant another year's worth of new recruits who would be cut before him, or sent to the front if needed. It was a selfish thought, he realized that, yet it was reality. He needed this job as much as any other man, more than the fresh recruits who didn't have families to support.

This was war, in more ways than one.

He glanced at Stadler, staring after the truck, and wondered how the young man would feel if he were to lose his job, or be sent to the front.

He'd hate the former, probably love the latter.

Though as indoctrinated as the boy was, he had chosen to be a police officer rather than a soldier. That spoke volumes as to how deep his convictions truly went. He'd serve the Reich by supporting it through his words, not his actions. He wasn't willing to put his life on the line.

"What now?"

Vogel flinched, his train of thought having taken him far from reality. "What?"

"I said, what now?"

"We begin knocking on doors."

Stadler checked his watch and grunted. "That's going to piss off a lot of people."

Vogel shrugged. "True, but someone may have heard something that could lead us to the perpetrator."

"I don't see how. They might have heard the gunshot, but they wouldn't have seen anything. It was blackout conditions."

Vogel headed for the nearest residential building. "There might have been an argument. A motive might have been uttered. A name. Anything. Or someone might have heard their neighbor returning at an odd hour. Anything is possible."

Stadler caught up to his senior partner's long stride. "I suppose you're right. But everyone would have been returning from the shelters. Proving they killed someone will be impossible unless they confess."

Vogel shook his head. "Perhaps, though you're forgetting two things."

"What's that?"

"Our victim was shot. You don't just toss a perfectly good weapon away if you're willing to kill. You keep that."

Stadler stepped ahead and pulled open the door to the first apartment building. "And the second?"

"They stole his clothes. There was a reason for that. They intended to keep them, perhaps to sell, perhaps to wear."

"Or maybe they wanted to hide who he was."

Vogel stopped, smiling at the first useful thought his partner had had all evening. "Very good thinking, Otto. We might just make a detective out of you yet." He climbed the first flight of stairs. "And *that's* why we need those fibers analyzed. If he was wearing some sort of uniform, we might be able to match it up with other clothes that the murderer took."

"Do you think he's military?"

"Perhaps, though that would be pretty ballsy. It's more likely, *if* he was wearing a uniform, that it's some other uniformed service. So many people wear uniforms these days, it's a wonder the shops even carry civilian clothes anymore. So many of the children run around in Hitler Youth uniforms now, it's hard to tell them apart."

Stadler stepped up to the first door. "He looked like he might have been the right age to be in the Hitler Youth."

Vogel rapped on the door. "Yes, he did. But let's hope you're wrong about that."

"Why?"

"Because then we're dealing with the murder of a child, not a man."

SS Reich Main Security Office

Niederkirchner Straße, Berlin, Nazi Germany

"How do you explain your failure?"

Konrad stood in front of General Graf's desk, his hands clasped behind his back, his chin high, his shoulders squared, and extremely disappointed the system hadn't yet found *him*. "I cannot, sir. We had scores of troops out searching for him, and they came up emptyhanded. Rest assured, we will continue the search until he is found and brought to justice."

Graf regarded him, a lone finger tapping on the ink blotter on his desk. "I've been told your son is missing as well."

Konrad tensed, his stomach churning. "Yes. My eldest, Joachim."

"Do you think the disappearances are connected?"

He dared not tell the man the truth. If it were revealed that Joachim had been the one who had taken the shot, it could be the end for the poor boy. He had to leave the general convinced it was Griese that was responsible. "No, not directly. I believe he may have been frightened by the combination of the air raid and the excitement surrounding the shot. I'm sure he'll turn up eventually, scared and hungry." He forced a smile. "And a little embarrassed, I'm sure."

"Cowards run in the face of danger."

Konrad stiffened. "He's only sixteen."

"Any good German should be ready to fight and die for the Reich at that age. And should he be called upon to serve the Führer, we can't have him and his ilk running away at the sound of the first gunshot."

Konrad's fingernails dug into the palm of his hand. "Of course not."

Graf flicked his wrist, dismissing him. "Your twenty-four hours are running out." The general's eyes bored into Konrad's. "And I assure you, Colonel, you don't want me investigating you and your obviously deficient family."

The blood drained from Konrad's cheeks and he snapped to attention. "Understood, sir." He hastily exited the general's office, his heart hammering, his cheeks suddenly flush with anger and fear. If the general unleashed his hounds on his family, they would undoubtedly discover their secret, and it would be the end for all of them, he was certain. He had worked hard over the years to track down every scrap of evidence he could find and destroy it, however there were still documents out there that could ruin them if they were found and linked back to his family.

They were a single detailed records search away from the firing squad.

I have to find Griese.

His thoughts had been dominated by his son's disappearance, but as horrible as it sounded, Griese was a bigger concern. He had barely thirteen hours before their lives were over. They would just have to pray that their son returned home on his own volition, and didn't reveal what he had discovered.

He left the building, rushing down the steps and into the back of his waiting car, his mind racing as to what more he could do. He had power. After all, he was a colonel in the SS. It gave him options that most wouldn't have, yet with each one exercised, it brought more attention to him and his family.

Attention they could ill afford.

Kriminalpolizei Headquarters

Prinz-Albrecht Straße, Berlin, Nazi Germany

"You sound tired."

Vogel grunted at his wife's observation as he leaned back in his chair, his eyes closed and burning. "You have no idea. We were out all night knocking on doors. Do you realize how upset people get in the middle of the night when you do that?"

"I can only imagine. When will you be home?"

He frowned. "No idea. We're about to go see the medical examiner."

"Do you have any idea who he was?"

"None. He was young though. Tragic."

"Somebody has to do something about these looters. If this keeps up, people are going to stay home to protect their property instead of seeking shelter. People are going to die."

"Otto thinks we should shoot them on sight."

"He might be right."

Vogel chuckled. "I'd tell him you said so, but I think he'd be stunned to find out I thought someone might not agree with him."

She laughed. "Will you be home for dinner? Remember, the Langs are supposed to be coming. I'd really like to make an effort to get to know them better. After all, they are our neighbors."

He cursed. "I forgot all about that." He sighed. "I'll try."

"Please do. Hermann was so bored last time when you couldn't make it."

He laughed, a smile spreading. "I guess I better try hard, then. If I miss a second one, we'll never get him to agree to come over again." He leaned forward. "Keep the plans. I'll try to be there."

"Good. Love you."

"Love you." He hung up the phone then rose as Stadler entered the office, two coffees in hand. Vogel took one then a sip. "This coffee is shit."

"I think the Panzer crews use it when they run out of petrol."

Vogel took another sip. "I can barely keep my eyes open."

"Me neither. If you had let me rough up some of those witnesses, we might have at least got something useful for our efforts."

Vogel shook his head then sat on the corner of his desk, nursing his caffeine injection. "You'll learn over time that when you rough up a suspect, they'll quite often tell you what they think you want to hear. Especially witnesses. We could be sent on wild goose chases because someone tells us they saw or heard something when they didn't."

Stadler frowned at him. "Sometimes I wonder how you ever became a cop. You're such a pacifist."

Vogel chuckled, finishing his coffee, already enjoying its effects. "We're not soldiers, son. We're police officers. The public shouldn't fear us."

"Then what's the point? We're not out there to make friends."

"No, but we *are* out there to protect the innocent. Criminals should fear us because we do our jobs well, and the public should help us because they want to, not because they're scared into it. Leave that crap to the Gestapo. We're the Kripo. We serve the people."

"We serve Adolf Hitler."

Vogel headed for the door, deciding the conversation was about to take a turn for the worse. "Let's go see what the medical examiner has to say. I want to know if those fibers revealed anything."

Berlin-Mitte Morgue

Hannoversche Straße, Berlin, Nazi Germany

"So, Doc, what have you got for us?"

Medical Examiner Hans Naumann glanced up from his microscope, squinting at the new arrivals. "Detective Vogel and his young partner. I would have thought you'd have gone home for some much-needed rest. From what I hear, you had half the force out last night knocking down doors."

Stadler jerked a thumb at Vogel. "Hardly. He wouldn't let us."

Naumann chuckled as he grabbed a file from his lab table. "Well, you should see yourselves. You look like death warmed over." He gestured at the tables behind him, half a dozen bodies on display. "And I know what I'm talking about."

Vogel frowned at the sight. "Busy night?"

"It's always busy when there's an air raid. And these are only the ones we can't say definitively died as a result of it."

Stadler's eyes widened. "You mean they could all be murder victims?"

"Highly unlikely, though theoretically possible."

Stadler grinned at Vogel. "Homicide could be busy!"

Vogel eyed him. "You do realize you're getting excited over the fact innocent people are dead."

Stadler shrugged. "We all have to die sometime. Might as well make someone's life interesting in the process."

Vogel rolled his eyes. "It's a good thing your father is so high up in the Party."

Stadler flushed, never happy when his parental connections were mentioned. It was well-known the only reason he was a police officer, and a detective already, was because his father had found him the position so he could avoid the front, despite Stadler's potential wishes to the contrary. "Why?"

"Because no one would dare teach you a lesson in civility."

Naumann snorted. "Ahh to be young and stupid." He shook the file held in his hand. "Your man last night was an interesting one."

"Any idea who he is?"

Naumann shook his head. "Not yet, beyond that he was murdered, and not a victim of the Allied bombers."

"I think the gunshot wound to his back kind of gave that away."

"It could have been shrapnel."

"In the shape of a bullet."

"All right, wise ass, do you want to give the briefing?"

Vogel grinned. "I wouldn't want to step on your toes, my friend."

Naumann grunted. "Maybe someone should teach *you* a lesson." His eyes narrowed as he tilted his head forward in an exaggerated manner. "Is *your* father anyone of importance?"

Vogel chuckled. "Nope. Swing away."

Naumann laughed, flipping open the file. "Well, you were right, he was shot in the back. I pulled a nine millimeter round out of him. But, he was also shot in the ear."

Vogel's eyes widened slightly. "The ear? How could you tell it wasn't just a rat bite?"

"First, there were no teeth marks, and second, it was close range, small caliber. Made a nice little hole in the cartilage. He was probably bleeding quite profusely before he was shot the second time."

Vogel scratched the back of his neck. "So, someone shot at him, hit him in the ear with a small-caliber weapon, then he turned to run, and he was shot in the back with a larger caliber weapon."

"Two shooters?" offered Stadler.

Vogel agreed. "It has to be. Only cowboys in American Westerns shoot with two guns at once." He turned to Naumann. "Any idea what caliber weapon made the first shot?"

"No, but judging by the hole, I'd say something like a twenty-two. But, just to correct you, I didn't say that was the first shot."

"Can't you tell?"

"Not really. If I had to hazard a guess, I'd say he was shot in the ear, then the back. How much time elapsed between the two shots, I can't say. If he was dressed, we might have been able to tell by the amount of blood on his clothes, but because he was naked, most of the blood that would have come from his ear was probably on his shirt or jacket. It could have been seconds, it could have been hours. I just can't say."

Vogel sighed. "Well, what we do know from what you told us, is that there were likely two shooters, though they could have been together."

Stadler looked at him. "Could? What are the chances of one guy getting shot by two different people at two different times on the same night?"

Naumann tilted his head. "He's got a point."

Vogel hated to admit when his partner was right, though his gut was telling him not to rush to judgment. "We have to find out who the hell this guy was. What can you tell me?"

"Young, sixteen to twenty, I'd say, by all appearances healthy and well-fed, a couple of old scars, probably childhood injuries, and no tattoos. I've sent his description and prints to Central Records. Hopefully they'll have an answer shortly."

Vogel's eyebrows shot up. "Oh? You sound confident. Millions of records to search, and you think they'll be able to identify him 'shortly?'"

Naumann smiled. "Well, I did have one little piece of information that will help narrow down the search considerably."

Vogel's heart rate ticked up in anticipation. "You found something in the gunshot wound, didn't you?"

Naumann pointed at the microscope he had been peering through when they arrived. "A piece of fabric was embedded in the wound, lodged in there by the bullet."

Vogel and Stadler exchanged excited glances. "And?"

"It's part of a uniform."

Stadler's eyes widened. "Hitler Youth?"

Naumann eyed him. "Why would you say that?"

Stadler shrugged. "He's young."

Naumann shook his head. "That's an amazing guess, my boy."

Stadler beamed.

"But you're completely wrong."

Vogel chuckled, always enjoying seeing his partner embarrassed by someone other than himself. "All right, wise guy, what kind of uniform was it?"

All humor disappeared from Naumann's face. "SS."

Vogel tensed, the entire nature of the case suddenly changing. "Are you certain?"

"I've triple checked. It's definitely part of an SS uniform."

Vogel pursed his lips as he folded his arms. "So, I assume you've told Central Records to search for SS personnel stationed in Berlin?"

"Yes. And if they've been reported missing, that should be a very short list. This isn't the front."

Vogel sighed. "Indeed." He stared at the microscope. "Anything else to tell us?"

Naumann shook his head. "Not at the moment. I'll let you know as soon as I hear something."

"Do that." Vogel turned and headed out of the morgue, Stadler following him, even the young man subdued.

"What do we do now?"

"We find out who he is."

Stadler eyed him. "What? Don't we have to wait for Central Records?"

Vogel shook his head at the daftness of his partner. "Think about it. What was going on last night while we were examining the body?"

Stadler stared at him blankly then his eyes shot wide. "The SS were swarming the area, searching for someone!"

"Exactly. And don't you think it's too much of a coincidence that our victim just happened to be in an SS uniform?"

Stadler held open the door for his senior partner. "So, our victim is who they were looking for."

"Exactly. And they obviously know who they were looking for, so we just need to meet with the right person, and we'll have our answer shortly."

"Who do we ask?"

Vogel shrugged. "I've always thought you should start at the top then work your way down."

Stadler's eyes bulged. "Are you kidding me? You intend to ask Himmler?"

Vogel chuckled as he climbed in their car. "Like I said, I've always *thought* you should. In practice, in today's Germany, it's rarely a good idea."

"Then how are we going to find out?"

"I suggest we head back to the scene and ask one of our fellow SS officers under whose orders they're operating, then ask him."

"You've got balls."

Vogel shrugged as he pulled away from the morgue. "For now. Let's hope they don't get snipped for asking the wrong questions of the wrong person."

Strausberger Straße

Berlin, Nazi Germany

Vogel parked the car behind one of their mobile units, the uniformed officer he had left in charge waving at them. Vogel climbed out and strode over to the small group of men, staring enviously at the green uniform he had once worn proudly.

Mornings were much easier back then.

"Anything?"

Sergeant Hellwig shook his head. "Not much, I'm afraid. We did get reports from some residents backing onto the alleyway that they heard gunshots during the air raid."

"Gun*shots*?"

Hellwig nodded. "Yes. Some said two, others said three."

"The medical examiner said he found two gunshot wounds in the victim, but from two different weapons."

Hellwig's eyebrows rose. "Really? Two shooters?"

"That's the assumption we're operating under."

"That sounds like looters, then. A crime of passion or targeted shooting is usually a single shooter."

Stadler ventured a supporting statement. "And a lone gunman in a hurry usually doesn't strip his victim naked."

Vogel agreed. "Two would definitely make it more expedient, but the alley is out of sight, especially during an air raid where it would be pitch black, and people are less likely to be near their glass windows."

Stadler folded his arms. "So, you're not ruling out the lone gunman theory?"

Hellwig eyed them both. "I thought you said there were two different weapons involved?"

Stadler jerked a thumb at Vogel. "He thinks he might have been shot once, then later shot again by a different person."

Hellwig smiled. "Did you cook that theory up after the schnapps?"

Vogel chuckled. "It's a long shot, I agree, but until I have proof either way, I'm not willing to dismiss it. However, the neighbors hearing multiple shots certainly suggests two people at a minimum are involved."

Stadler stared down the alleyway. "Did they say if the shots sounded the same?"

Hellwig turned to the young detective. "Excuse me?"

"Did they sound the same? We're dealing with two different caliber weapons here. If the shots sounded different, then likely both wounds were inflicted at the same time. But if they sounded the same, then one of the wounds might have been from earlier."

Vogel gave a wry smile. "An astute observation." He turned to Hellwig. "Well?"

Hellwig flushed as he made a show of flipping through his notes, exchanging glances with the other officers, everyone shrugging or avoiding eye contact. Hellwig finally gave up, squaring his shoulders. "We'll go back and ask."

"Do that." Vogel pointed at the SS at the top of the street. "Any idea who they're looking for?"

"Nope. They don't talk to us, we don't talk to them."

Vogel sighed. "Well, I have a feeling they're looking for our victim, but are too arrogant to ask."

Stadler sucked in a rather loud breath and Vogel rolled his eyes for Hellwig's benefit.

"Find out about those shots, Sergeant, then let me know." He paused. "Oh, and let's try to keep this off the radios as much as possible. I don't want our case being taken away sooner than it has to be."

Hellwig smiled. "Messengers it is." He gestured toward the nearest apartment and his men went to work as Vogel walked up the slight incline toward a checkpoint manned by SS guards.

"You really need to be careful who you're insulting the SS in front of. You could get yourself placed in protective custody, and you know what that means."

Vogel glanced over his shoulder at his partner. "Who's going to tell them? You?"

Stadler's eyes bulged. "No, I mean, of course not, but, well, what if one of the others reported it, then I was asked? I can't lie! Not to the SS!"

Vogel regarded the pale-faced young man. "No, *you* shouldn't. They'd suspect you in a heartbeat and you'd never see the light of day again. The rest of us are capable of deciding for ourselves what truths should be told."

"Who are we to decide that?"

Vogel stopped and turned to face Stadler. "You mean you would condemn a man to death simply because he called the SS arrogant, when to save his life, all you'd need to do was say you don't recall the man saying anything of the sort, though you might be mistaken?"

Stadler stared at him, his mouth agape. "Well, when you put it that way, I guess not, but I don't think I'd be able to come up with that so quickly." He paused, stealing a glance at the checkpoint. "Or believably."

Vogel grunted then slapped him on the shoulder. "Practice in front of the mirror at night. These days, one must always be prepared for the unexpected."

"I-I suppose."

Vogel resumed the trek, raising a hand of greeting to the squad leader in charge. "Kriminalinspektor Vogel. Who's your Commanding Officer?"

"*Untersturmführer* Jander."

"Where is he?"

The squad leader's eyes drifted to the ground for a moment. "He's, umm, in the bakery." He gestured toward the building across the street.

Vogel spotted the lieutenant leaning against the counter inside, chatting up a beautiful example of Aryan breeding. "Perhaps to save your CO some embarrassment, you should fetch him."

The man's eyes flared for a moment before he clicked his heels. "Yes, sir!" He rushed into the bakery and moments later a none-too-pleased Jander emerged, straightening his hat. He marched over, hands clasped behind his back, chin jutted out, his eyes inquisitively assessing who would dare interrupt his rutting. The man came to a halt in front of Vogel, uncomfortably in his personal space.

"The meaning for this interruption?"

"I'm Kriminalinspektor Vogel."

"So? Do you honestly believe your business is of any interest to the SS?"

Vogel smiled slightly. "Since we're *all* SS, then my business is your business."

The man grunted. "You are SS in command structure only. To classify yourself as one of us is laughable."

Vogel spotted Stadler nearly pissing himself in fright nearby.

Keep it together, kid.

"Perhaps it will be necessary to tell your commanding officer what I know, since you're apparently not interested."

Jander's nostrils flared and Vogel sensed a crack in the arrogance. He glanced toward the large windows of the bakery, the cute blonde standing there, watching the proceedings, a fact the young officer was likely aware of.

He was putting on a show.

And it was about to backfire if he didn't stop pushing so hard.

Jander took a step back. "I don't think that will be necessary. We wouldn't want to waste his time with trivial matters, now would we?"

Vogel suppressed the smile of victory, and much to the horror of his partner, decided to have a little fun with it. "Actually, I think this information *is* of too much importance for a mere lieutenant. Who is your commander?"

There was a gulp. "Colonel Konrad."

"And where might I find him?"

"I believe he is at his residence. His son is missing."

This caught Vogel off guard. Could these men be merely searching for a wayward youth? Perhaps they weren't looking for their victim at all? Perhaps they didn't even know an SS member had been murdered last night. "His son?"

"Joachim Konrad. Sixteen years old. Missing since an incident last night involving…"

"Involving?"

"Involving Corporal Griese, a member of the Colonel's personal staff."

"And what was this incident?"

"We haven't been informed of that, sir. We are merely tasked with finding both."

"And was Corporal Griese in uniform when he went missing?"

Jander's eyes narrowed. "I'm…not sure. I believe he was on duty at the time, so I would assume so."

Vogel frowned. "Then I definitely need to see your commanding officer."

The man paled slightly. "Why?"

"Because I believe we have the man you're looking for."

Jander appeared hopeful. "You have him in custody?"

Vogel shook his head. "No. We have him in the morgue."

Berlin-Mitte Morgue

Hannoversche Straße, Berlin, Nazi Germany

Medical Examiner Naumann wiped his hands dry then picked up the phone demanding attention on his desk. "Naumann."

"This is Holz from Central Records. I have a match for one of your bodies." A reference number was rattled off.

"Give me a moment." He flipped through the stack of files on his desk and fished out the one in question. His eyebrows shot up when he saw who it was. "I just sent this in. You've IDed him already?"

"Yes. Corporal Klaus Griese. Second SS Infantry Brigade, part of Colonel Rudolph Konrad's personal staff. He's deceased."

Naumann rolled his eyes, glancing at the body not five meters from where he was standing. "No, really?"

"Yes. Died in the air raid last night."

Naumann's eyes narrowed. "You mean he died *during* the air raid last night."

"No, *in*. According to the official record, he died as a result of the bombings. Killed when the building he was in collapsed after it was hit by a downed enemy bomber."

Naumann dropped into his chair, his body tense. Something was wrong here. It was likely a clerical error, though Central Records prided themselves on making few of those. "I think there's been a mistake."

There was a pause, offense about to be taken. "What makes you say that?"

"The man I sent the prints on is lying in my morgue, with a gunshot wound to the back, and no evidence of injuries from a building collapse."

The pause was longer this time. "That's impossible."

"Well, all I can tell you is that if the prints match, then there's a problem. This man did not die because of the air raid, and I can't see how anyone identified him, because he's been here all night with only myself to keep him company."

"But that's impossible."

Naumann growled. "Why do you keep saying that?"

And when he heard, his stomach flipped as his ears pounded with fear.

What have I got myself mixed up in?

Konrad Residence

Berlin, Nazi Germany

Maximilian stood near the door, pressed against the wall, peering into the next room, his breath held. His father's aide, Captain Hoffman, was kneeling near the fireplace, a bundle of something in his hands. The man glanced over his shoulder, as if to check if he were alone, and Maximilian jerked his head back, his heart hammering.

He listened, then heard the fireplace screen scrape on the hearth. He inched his head toward the opening and finally caught sight of Hoffman once again, and his eyes bulged. His father's aide poked at something now roaring in the fire, something that appeared to be clothing.

Black clothing.

A uniform!

He gasped. Hoffman's head whipped around and Maximilian spun, scurrying away as his little feet pounded on the hardwood floors then up the stairs. He rushed into his bedroom and slammed the door shut before diving onto his bed and burying himself under his blanket. He grabbed his pillow, pulling it under the covers with him, and hugged it hard as he strained to hear anything over the pounding of his heart.

And he heard nothing.

Then footfalls.

His heart hammered even harder.

He could hear them now, slowly walking down the hallway, approaching his door.

They stopped.

As almost did his drumming heart.

He had never been so afraid in his life. He had seen something he shouldn't. He had seen Hoffman burning a uniform. An SS uniform. Why, he had no idea, but he could think of no good reason someone would burn a uniform.

The doorknob squeaked.

It was a squeak that had always annoyed him. He could never sneak out of his room at night without someone hearing it, so he hadn't bothered in ages.

But this time the squeak worked to his advantage.

The knob stopped turning, Hoffman obviously hesitating.

"What should I do?"

"Scream."

He flinched at Frida's harsh whisper, then pressed his ear against the wall. "What if they don't hear me?"

"You don't have a choice. He's going to kill you."

"Are-are you sure?"

"Why else would he follow you? He's obviously mad. What did you do?"

"I was spying."

"Again?"

"What else am I supposed to do? I'm so bored."

"What did you see?"

"I saw him burning an SS uniform."

The doorknob squeaked again.

He cringed. "He's coming."

"You have to scream."

"If he kills me, will you tell my parents' that I love them?"

"I-I can't."

His eyes burned at the thought of never seeing them again. "Why not?"

The door opened and he held his breath, praying Frida didn't say anything that might give away the fact she knew what was going on. Despite her refusals, she might still do the right thing should he not survive the next few moments.

The doorbell rang, and the footsteps approaching his bed stopped. Somebody downstairs rushed toward the door then he heard a muffled exchange before feet pounded on the stairs.

And inside his room, Hoffman retreated back through the doorway, the knob squeaked, and the door shut.

And Maximilian remained shaking in his bed, wondering what to do.

I wish Joachim was here!

Konrad Residence

Berlin, Nazi Germany

"I'm concerned about Maximilian."

Renata turned toward her husband, the fussing with her wiry hair momentarily forgotten. "What do you mean?"

Konrad exhaled loudly as he checked his collar in the mirror, already regretting adding to his wife's burdens. "I caught him talking to Frida in his bedroom."

His wife paled slightly, a hand darting to her mouth. "But he mustn't!"

He frowned. "You don't think I know that?"

"What did you say to him?"

"I told him to stop talking to his imaginary friend. Then I told him I had one too when I was his age."

"You encouraged him?"

He gave her a look. "I tried to comfort our crying son. What would you have me say?"

"You tell him he's too old to have imaginary friends and that he should forget about her."

He sat beside his wife, taking her hand in his. "You know as well as I do that a boy that age will never obey such a command. The more we attempt to dissuade him from talking to her, the more he will latch on to her."

"But we must! If someone hears him speaking to her, your career could be over. Our sons could be ostracized. We could lose everything, perhaps even our lives."

She was right. And hearing his young son utter Frida's name had been gut-wrenching in more ways than one. But Maximilian was too young to risk explaining the danger to, for it would be an even greater danger should he repeat their secret to someone he thought he could trust, then be betrayed.

For there was no one under this roof that he trusted besides his wife. Even his eldest couldn't be trusted. Not with the secrets this family held. Not in this country in these difficult times.

He closed his eyes, his shoulders slumping.

His wife squeezed the back of his neck. "What is it?"

"It's all unravelling on us, isn't it? We were fools to think we could keep everything hidden. We should have left when we had the chance."

She rested her head on his shoulder. "There's no point dwelling on past decisions. We're here today, and we have to deal with it. If it weren't for the boys, I would shout the truth from the rooftops just so it could all be over, but we have to do everything we can to save them. They're completely innocent in this."

He sighed, staring into her eyes. "Joachim will probably be the death of us all."

Her face clouded with fear. "We should never have let them have him. We should never have let him join the Hitler Youth. He used to be such a good boy. Now he's a tyrant in his own home."

He grunted. "An SS senior officer with a teenage son who isn't in the Hitler Youth? If that didn't raise flags, nothing would." He flopped down on the bed, his wife joining him in staring at the canopy overhead. "And you saw how excited he was about joining. There would have been no stopping him."

"We're his parents."

"We're his parents, yes, but back then, he still remembered. He still knew."

She rolled over on her side, placing a hand on his chest. "And now that he's seen the photo, it's obviously all coming back to him."

"If we could only find him. I could tell him a story, one that he just might believe enough to cast doubt, enough to stop him from telling the authorities. We just need to find him, get a chance to talk to him before anyone else."

"I don't see that happening unless he comes home on his own accord."

He frowned, rolling onto his side and embracing her, his eyes burning, his chest aching as he took in the beauty that was the woman he had fallen in love with all those years ago. A woman so vulnerable, so in constant fear, a woman that hid everything so well for his sake and that of the children, that he sometimes forgot the truth that dominated their lives. "We'll find him. He's a good boy. He'll come to his senses. He's just in shock."

She patted his cheek, a tear rolling down hers. "You're just saying that to make me feel better."

He smiled. "Is it working?"

She held him tight, her shoulders heaving, her answer revealed.

A knock at the outer door of their bedchambers had them both flinching. He extricated himself and they both rolled from the bed, his wife quickly to her vanity to straighten her hair and makeup in case her presence was required, and he to his mirror to straighten his uniform. He grabbed his jacket off the back of the chair and shoved his arms inside before straightening the collar.

He checked his wife who nodded, then opened the outer door to find Hoffman standing there, fidgeting as if nervous about something. "What is it?"

An identification card was handed over. "A Kriminalinspektor Vogel is here to see you, sir. Apparently, he has information you must hear."

Konrad frowned as he checked the ID. "What information?"

"He refused to say."

"He refused?"

"Yes, sir."

Konrad shook his head. "The impudence is galling. Where is he?"

"I had him and his partner shown to the drawing room."

"Very well. I'll be there in a moment."

"Yes, sir."

Konrad closed the door as the crisp footfalls of his aide faded down the hall.

"What is it?"

Konrad turned to see his wife standing in the doorway to their bedroom. "A detective is here from the Kripo."

Her eyes widened and her hand darted to her flushed chest. "Do you think…"

He held up a finger. "I don't know what to think. It could have nothing to do with last night. Let me go deal with this. You stay here."

She nodded. "As you wish."

He sighed. "You know what I mean."

She waved her hand. "I know, that wasn't fair. And you're right. In my state, I'm liable to raise suspicions. You go. If they ask of me, tell them I'm exhausted from being up all night and am taking a nap." She drew a deep breath. "It won't be that far from the truth."

He stepped over and gave her a quick peck on the cheek then headed for the salon. Hoffman opened the door for him and he strode inside, hands clasped behind his back, ever the model of perfect SS arrogance, despite his true feelings. "How may I be of assistance to the Kriminalpolizei today?"

The man in charge, around his age, large framed with a demeanor that suggested to him he was tired with a lot of things in his life, one of them likely the young partner he had with him, a man who appeared more Gestapo than Kripo. The man extended his hand. "I'm

Kriminalinspektor Vogel, sir, and this is my partner, *Kriminalassistent* Stadler."

"Colonel Konrad." He returned the identification Hoffman had provided. "What brings you here today?" He motioned toward several seats then took his preferred one.

Vogel sat, crossing his legs, his partner preferring to slowly meander about the room. "It is our understanding that you are searching for an SS corporal that went missing last night."

Konrad tensed. "Where did you hear that?"

"I have my sources."

He smiled slightly. "No doubt one of my men informed you. We keep nothing from our police brothers unless it's absolutely necessary. Yes, Corporal Griese abandoned his post last night. What has that to do with you?"

"We have a body in the morgue that I believe may be your missing man."

Konrad's heart rate picked up and he shifted in his chair. "What makes you think it's him?"

"He was found in the area, stripped naked, with two bullet wounds, one of which contained a scrap of an SS uniform. Was he in uniform when he disappeared?"

Konrad nodded.

"Then I suggest you, or someone familiar with his appearance, accompany me to the morgue so we can make a positive identification."

"Can't Central Records do that?"

"They're in the process right now, however that may take days or worse. For the sake of our investigation, it would be best if we knew now rather than later. The longer we wait, the less likely it is we will catch the murderer."

"Murderer?"

"He was found with two bullet wounds."

Konrad shook his head. "Yes, sorry, you mentioned that." Vogel regarded him with what he was certain was suspicion. He needed to put the man's mind at ease otherwise he might ask questions he wasn't prepared to answer. "I apologize, Detective, but our eldest son is missing, and I find myself rather preoccupied."

Vogel leaned forward, concern on his face. "Yes, that was also mentioned by my…source. When did he go missing?"

"Since around the same time, as a matter of fact. He had been chastised along with his brother earlier in the evening, and I fear he ran away from the embarrassment. I'm hoping he will return home shortly, though as a father, I'm of course fearing the worst."

"I understand. I have two children myself. How old is your boy?"

"Sixteen."

Vogel wrote in his notebook. "And his name?"

"Joachim."

"What was he wearing?"

"His Hitler Youth uniform."

The partner paused his perusal of the room, glancing at Vogel who ignored him.

"What does he look like?"

"Tall for his age, good build, dark hair, dark eyes."

Vogel nodded. "I'll put the word out with our men to keep an eye out for any wayward Hitler Youth matching his description." He regarded Konrad for a moment. "Do you think the disappearances are related in any way? Could Griese have taken him?"

Konrad hesitated. If he told this man the truth about last night's events, it could spell trouble for them all. If he told them the *perceived* truth, the truth General Graf believed, then it would mean even more people would be aware of the embarrassing events.

Yet the body in the morgue had to be Griese, didn't it? There couldn't possibly be two missing SS members in the same area, could there?

"Detective, I assume I can count on your discretion?"

Vogel's eyes darted toward his partner. "Yes, you can count on *my* discretion."

The emphasis was subtle, and if he hadn't noticed the sideways glance at the young partner, he might have missed it.

Yet it was perfectly understood.

He turned in his chair. "Stadler, was it?"

Stadler snapped to attention, facing Konrad. "Yes, sir."

"Would you do me a favor? My men aren't trained investigators like you are. Would you mind going outside and taking a look around the grounds, see if there's anything we might have missed that might suggest where my son or my corporal might have gone?"

Stadler's chest swelled and he turned to Vogel. "With your permission, sir?"

Vogel flicked his wrist toward the door. "Go. I'll meet you outside."

Stadler bowed his head at both of them, then left the room. Konrad waited for the footfalls to fade before leaning forward in his chair, Vogel doing the same.

"There was an incident here last night, but it must not become general knowledge, if you know what I mean."

Vogel flipped his notebook closed. "You have my word I will not repeat anything you tell me unless it becomes vitally necessary to solve my case."

Konrad pursed his lips. The answer was as honest as it could be, which was unfortunate. He would have felt better if the man had simply promised he would never repeat what he was about to hear, and leave it at that. But this Vogel was obviously a dedicated officer, and if honorable, would likely keep to himself the information about to be revealed unless it indeed became necessary.

Why else would he have indicated his partner should leave the room?

"There was a shooting here during a formal dinner party last night."

Vogel's eyebrows rose and he leaned back in his chair. "Was anyone injured?"

Konrad shook his head. "No. The shooter missed."

"Who was the target?"

"I don't know. There were many high ranking officers here. The guest list is confidential for the moment, however, suffice it to say that I was by no means the highest-ranked officer here."

"Was Corporal Griese the shooter?"

Konrad forced his answer as quickly as he could, not risking any hesitation in his voice. "Yes."

"You saw him take the shot?"

"No. The shot came from outside. The window shattered, I rushed over to it and spotted Griese standing there. The gen—one of the guests shouted at him and he ran. He hasn't been seen since."

Vogel's head bobbed, his lips jutting out. "So, your corporal shot at your dinner party, fled, and *if* he is the man in our morgue, was then shot twice, by two different weapons."

"Two?"

"A small caliber weapon inflicted a wound to the corporal's ear, then a larger caliber weapon was used to shoot him in the back. It's not clear if both wounds were suffered around the same time, though there is evidence to suggest they might have been."

Konrad hid his concern. He had hoped his son had missed, and it was indeed glass that had injured Griese, but now that it was confirmed his son had shot the Corporal, questions were already being asked. These detectives might not rest until they identified *both* shooters. He had already revealed more than he wanted, but he had to keep his son out of this. No one could know he had fired the shot.

And this all but confirmed the body Vogel was referring to was indeed Griese.

Which posed even bigger problems.

Konrad rose. "I think the best way to move this investigation along is to confirm who you have in your morgue. If it isn't Griese, then we can both move on with our respective tasks. If it is, then my job is finished, but yours has just begun."

Vogel rose. "Agreed."

Konrad led them out of the house and Stadler flagged them down.

"Sir, I think I found something."

Konrad tensed, but allowed Vogel to deal with his underling.

"What is it?"

"Blood."

Konrad Residence

Berlin, Nazi Germany

"Blood?" Vogel noticed Konrad bristle at the word before quickly recovering his composure. "Does that surprise you, Colonel?"

Konrad shook his head, though said nothing. His nostrils flared and he finally nodded. "Was it near the window at the side of the house, looking into the dining room?"

Stadler shrugged. "It's over on this side, yes. There's a boarded-up window there. I don't know what's on the other side."

Konrad held out his arm, indicating the way. "That's the window I told you about, Detective. Shattered in the incident. When I saw the…individual in question, he had a head wound. I assume the glass fell on him when it shattered."

Vogel listened, but said nothing, the words delivered with relieved glee. They rounded the corner and Stadler pointed at the ground, what could be dried blood evident, along with a severely disturbed crime scene, the workers dealing with the window thoroughly destroying any hope of performing a proper investigation.

Vogel knelt and ran his fingers over the dark patch, the dew still present in the shaded area coming away red. "Definitely could be blood." He glanced up at the boarded window then rose, reaching up to touch the sill. "And the dining room is on the other side of that?"

"Yes."

Vogel wiped his fingers on his handkerchief. "Interesting."

Konrad stared at him. "What?"

Vogel kept his suspicions to himself.

"Our body at the morgue didn't have any wounds on him that would be caused by glass."

Vogel suppressed the glare he wanted to deliver to Stadler.

The boy needs to know when to shut up.

Konrad regarded him. "Is this true?"

Vogel nodded. "Yes. There were two gunshot wounds, then minor wounds caused by vermin."

Konrad clasped his hands behind his back, a curt nod delivered. "Then that settles it. The man in the morgue can't be Corporal Griese. Griese absolutely had a head wound when I saw him, and it could only have been caused by the glass when it shattered from the shot he fired." Konrad turned on his heel, heading for the front of the house. "I hope you'll forgive me, Detective, however I must concern myself with the search for my son, and for Corporal Griese. I don't have time to waste going to the morgue to identify a body I know not to be my missing corporal."

Vogel frowned, but decided protesting the decision would be fruitless, and perhaps dangerous. "I understand, Colonel. May I call upon you again should something of importance come up?"

Konrad waved a hand over his shoulder before disappearing around the corner. "Of course, of course."

Vogel turned toward Stadler. "You need to button that lip when you're around witnesses or potential suspects."

Stadler's eyes narrowed. "Suspects?"

Vogel jabbed a finger after the colonel. "I wanted him to come in and confirm who we have. Now, because you gave him a way out of that, we have to wait for Central Records. We could have saved days."

"But it isn't Corporal Griese. We just confirmed that."

Vogel sighed. "Have we?"

Stadler stared at him. "Haven't we? He was cut by falling glass. Our guy doesn't have any wounds from glass."

"What if he was shot here?"

Stadler's eyes widened. "Huh?"

"The body was stripped naked. That means he wasn't just shot and left there. Time was taken to disguise who he was." Vogel pointed at the patch of blood. "What if he was shot right there, stripped naked, then his body dumped elsewhere?"

Stadler's mouth was agape. "Do you think that's what happened?"

"Of course not. If he did take a shot at a senior officer, shooting him would be completely justified, and nobody would question it nor try to hide that fact."

"Then why—"

"I was merely giving you an example of why the colonel could be a suspect. You need to learn to keep things to yourself, otherwise you let your suspect pool know what you know, and that gives them a chance to cover up other evidence we might not have found yet."

"So, the colonel is just a witness."

"Yes, and one who is under extreme stress with the disappearance of his son, though I fear he has more to be worried about concerning someone under his command trying to kill one of his houseguests." He headed for the front of the house and their car. "Let's get the description of his son out to everyone, then check our messages. Maybe the guys have some more details on the gunshots."

Berlin-Mitte Morgue

Hannoversche Straße, Berlin, Nazi Germany

Naumann stared at the paperwork brought in minutes ago, confirming what Central Records had reported. The man on his table was indeed Corporal Griese. The photos matched.

And the records also indicated the man was reported deceased *before* he had made his request for identification. And this wasn't the left hand not knowing what the right was doing. This wasn't one of Vogel's men making the request before he did.

This was something entirely different.

The incident report showed the man identified as Griese had been badly burned during the air raid, and that his identity papers were used to ID the body.

Naumann had the luxury of a body with a face, and there was no doubt in his mind that Griese was on his table, unless the man had a twin, and the records already confirmed he had no brothers. This *was*

Griese. And that begged the question: how did his identity papers end up on the body of a man who just happened to have his face badly burned?

The doors to the room swung open and Vogel entered with his partner. "Hey, Doc, I got a message you wanted to see me. Did you hear back from Central Records already?"

Naumann eyed the young partner, not thrilled with the prospect of theorizing in front of someone so dedicated to the cause when the SS were involved.

Vogel yawned. "Otto, why don't you track down some coffee for us, I'm dying here."

Stadler sighed then brightened as he pointed to a pot sitting on a table nearby. "What's wrong with that stuff?"

"It's shit. The Doc couldn't brew a decent pot of coffee if his life depended on it. And besides, would you want to drink something that was brewed in this room?"

This gave Stadler pause. "Yeah, you're right."

Naumann shrugged. "Fine, if my coffee isn't good enough for you, there's a place on the corner." He pointed at a carafe on the table. "Take that, say it's for me, they know how I like it."

"How's that?"

"Black."

Vogel grunted. "Is there any other choice these days?"

Stadler left, saying nothing, clearly displeased with the assigned duty. Vogel held up a finger for a moment, then went to the door, evidently not trusting his partner at all. "All right, Doc, why'd I just send my partner away?"

"I'll be quick." Naumann handed him the file from Central Records and Vogel flipped through it, frowning, his head shaking. "What's wrong?"

"This says our man is Corporal Griese."

"Exactly."

"But I've been assured that it can't be."

Naumann's eyes widened. "By whom?"

"His commanding officer, Colonel Konrad."

A chill ran down Naumann's spine. He took the file and flipped to the incident report concerning "Griese's" death. "Read this."

Vogel did, his eyes widening. He pointed at the bodies. "Which one is our victim?"

Naumann led him to the body and pulled back the sheet. Vogel held up the page containing his photo.

"This is definitely Griese."

Naumann covered him back up. "You know that, and I know that, but Central Records says a man died last night, badly burned including his face, and was found with our victim's identity papers with him. Don't you find that a little bit convenient? I mean, a badly burned face?"

Vogel nodded, handing back the file. "Well, here's something you don't know, that I just found out. According to his CO, our young corporal took a shot at his colonel's dinner party last night, shattering a window, and cutting himself on the falling glass."

Naumann tore the sheet off the body, quickly reconfirming what he already knew. "This man has no cuts."

"That's what I thought." He lowered his voice. "But here's the thing. We found blood outside the window where he took the shot."

Naumann's eyes widened. None of this was making sense. "A lot of blood?"

"No, certainly nothing to indicate he had died there, though the area was pretty trampled with workers dealing with the shattered window. It was Stadler's eagle eyes that spotted it."

"Wolfgang, what do you think is going on here? I mean, someone is lying, right? We know this is Griese. We can at least agree on that, right?"

"Yes."

"Then the colonel must be lying. This man did not suffer cuts from glass."

Vogel blew air out from between his lips, causing them to sputter. "There must be another explanation."

"Such as?"

"Well, we're assuming the man he saw bleeding outside the window was Griese."

"You're not suggesting he wouldn't recognize his own man?"

"I'm suggesting it was dark outside, he was in a well-lit room, a shot had just been fired, people were panicking, and whoever was outside that window, bleeding, ran away almost immediately. Perhaps he assumed it was Griese because he's now missing."

Naumann held his tongue. The theory was as good as any, though he wasn't buying it. It was just too much of a coincidence for Griese to go missing the same night as an assassination attempt on one of the colonel's house guests. "He'd recognize the uniform, wouldn't he?"

"Excuse me?"

"The uniform. He might not recognize the face, but he'd recognize the uniform. Whoever did this was in uniform. What are the chances of two NCOs being mixed up in two unrelated incidents on the same evening? Nil in my books."

Vogel's head bobbed slowly. "Agreed. I believe that Griese was the man at the window."

"But you just said—"

"I merely proposed a plausible alternative to the colonel lying."

Naumann frowned. "I suppose, but if you believe it was Griese, then you do agree the colonel was lying?"

Vogel shook his head. "I can think of another explanation."

"Do tell."

"The colonel wasn't lying, he was mistaken."

"About what?"

"Let's assume it was Griese, and that he was bleeding. Colonel Konrad believes that he was cut by falling glass." Vogel pointed at the ear with the small bullet hole through it. "I suggest he wasn't bleeding from a cut, but was bleeding from the bullet wound he had just received."

Naumann's eyes narrowed. "He shot himself in the ear?"

"No, he was shot by someone else."

"You mean he tried to be a hero and blocked the shot with his own head?"

Vogel chuckled. "Nooo, I mean someone was trying to shoot him, hit him in the ear, and the bullet went through the window, shattering the glass. The shooter ran away before the colonel reached the window to look out. All that was left was a bleeding Griese, who was immediately accused of being the shooter. He ran in a panic."

"Then who shot him in the back?"

"*That's* the question, now, isn't it?"

Naumann stared at the wounded ear. It would have bled profusely at first, and without any evidence to the contrary, the colonel could be forgiven for thinking he had been the shooter. And if that were the case, then the only possible explanation for the bleeding he would have witnessed would have been the glass.

Who would ever think that the shooter shot himself?

"Fine, I'll agree with you that this is a very likely explanation. There would be no need for the colonel to lie about seeing Griese bleeding. He would merely have said he saw Griese standing there, then the man ran. Why have him bleeding unless he actually was?"

"Exactly. So, *we* know Griese was shot in the ear, then the back, by two different weapons. Neither wound was self-inflicted, and if we assume he was indeed shot when the window shattered, then we know the two shootings were separate incidents."

"Right. So, he was shot in the ear, that person ran away. Griese was then seen, bleeding, and then ran away when challenged. He was then *later* shot in the back by a larger caliber weapon, likely *not* by the same shooter." Naumann shook his head. "This is one unlucky bastard."

Vogel grunted. "Agreed." He covered him again with the sheet. "There's another thing I noticed when I was at the colonel's residence."

"What's that?"

"The window was too high."

"Huh?"

"The window was too high. Now, when I was there, it was boarded up, but I had to reach above my shoulder to touch the sill. You'd have to be almost three meters tall to have a chance of hitting anyone sitting at a table inside."

Naumann exhaled slowly. "So, it wasn't an assassination attempt."

"Not of anyone in the party, at least. Griese could have been the target, or the shooter simply wanted to scare those inside by shooting out the window, and Griese happened to get in the way."

Naumann thought for a moment. "But that wouldn't make sense, unless they were a horrendous shot."

"What do you mean?"

He motioned at the body. "He's average height and was shot in the ear. The shooter, if he was targeting the window, would have shot at the center of it. To try and hit that target, and to have also hit Griese in the ear by accident, would mean the shooter would have to be a dwarf to have an upward angle like that."

Vogel smiled slightly. "You're right. I hadn't thought of that. So, that means Griese was the target all along, and the bullet went through his ear and hit the bottom of the window, shattering the entire thing."

"A reasonable theory?"

Vogel nodded. "Yes. And again, we come back to who was the shooter, and then who was the second shooter."

"They could still be one and the same."

"How?"

"Well, now that we know there was some time between the two shots, in theory, the shooter could have retrieved a second weapon to finish the job."

"Definitely possible." Vogel eyed him. "I think you missed your calling, Doc."

Naumann laughed, batting away the words with a wave of his hand. "Sorry, my place is here, yours is out there." He chuckled. "Though I do enjoy theorizing with you detectives."

"Well, if you ever change your mind, let me know."

"So, what are you going to do now?"

"Well, there's one big part of this that you forgot."

Naumann's eyes widened slightly. "What?"

"The reason you called me here."

Naumann gasped. "Oh my God, yes! The second body already identified as our man here. I can't believe I forgot about that."

Vogel smiled. "So, you've had more time to think about it than I have. What do *you* think is going on?"

Naumann frowned at being put on the spot. Yes, he had been thinking about it. Nothing but, though more in the context of what would happen to him if the wrong person found out he had discovered the deception. "Umm, well, I'm assuming Griese was killed, his body stripped to hide his identity, and his papers taken at that time. Whoever took these then partially burned them so his photo was no longer visible, went to the area where the bombings took place, found a suitable victim, dressed him in the uniform, and planted the papers on him. When the body was found, the ID was used to identify the body, and it was then processed through Central Records."

Vogel nodded. "That's exactly what I think happened as well. There's just one problem, however."

"What?"

"What were their plans when the real body was found and processed through Central Records?"

Naumann scratched his chin. "Hope everyone thought it was a clerical error?"

"Somebody somewhere would still be missing a body. Somebody would be wondering why their husband or son didn't come home and they weren't notified. There'd be an investigation, someone would eventually discover that there was a discrepancy with the identifications of two bodies, and the error corrected. Then somebody would be asking the same questions we would be."

Naumann sat in his chair, indicating Vogel should do the same across from him. "Whoever did this, must not have had time to deal with the real Griese. If he had disposed of the body, then none of this would be happening."

"Not the easiest thing to do, especially if you're alone and in a hurry. Our victim isn't exactly a sack of feathers. I'm guessing our killer tried to move him, realized he couldn't, so stripped him down instead and decided to plant the identity papers on another body."

"But why do that? You've killed him. Who cares if someone figures it out?"

"Perhaps his identity is a clue as to who the murderer is."

"So, what you're saying is he killed the guy, tried to hide his identity, made Central Records believe he died innocently during an air raid, then hoped what, that the other body would just disappear?"

Vogel shook his head. "No, I'm saying either he meant to come back and deal with the real Griese, or he didn't care if it was eventually discovered, he only cared that someone knew Griese was dead as quickly as possible."

Naumann regarded his friend. "That makes no sense at all."

Vogel grinned. "It doesn't, does it? This is what happens when I think out loud rather than to myself. All the idiotic stuff is heard."

Naumann sighed, pondering Vogel's words when something occurred to him. "Here's a thought. You've shot Griese in the back, so it's obviously murder. You can't go tell someone, hey, look over here, there's a body, because you're not supposed to be there."

Vogel leaned forward. "Go on."

"The problem is, you need someone to know he's dead for some reason, so you plant the papers on someone else that *will* be discovered in short order, then go back to wherever you came from to establish your alibi."

Vogel leaned back and folded his arms, his head slowly bobbing. "So, you shoot him, can't tell anyone, but you want the authorities to know for some reason, then you take his clothes and ID, find a dead body from the bombing, dress him, doctor the papers, knowing he'll be found during the cleanup. You head back home, and by the time the truth is known, you're either long gone, or have an alibi that's so tight, no one would dare question it, and with the passage of time, memories become fuzzy and you get away with murder."

Naumann shrugged. "What do you think?"

"I think there are some serious holes in that theory."

"Like what?"

"Well, why the time constraint?"

"What do you mean?"

"I mean, strip him naked, destroy his paperwork, then leave him to be found. It would take a day or two to identify the body normally, and you'd have the same situation. Enough of a delay for you to establish an alibi, and, more importantly, no questions posed as to why there are *two* Corporal Griese's dead in one night."

Naumann smiled slightly. "You mean he couldn't risk Griese not being found."

Vogel nodded. "Exactly. For some reason, he had to make sure someone thought Griese was dead, couldn't tell anyone where the real body was, so in desperation created the deception, figuring the consequences were worse if he didn't."

"But what could possibly motivate someone to do such a thing? What kind of time constraint could they be operating under?"

"Well, if you had seen how many SS troops were on the street last night, you wouldn't be asking that."

"There were a lot?"

"Hundreds. Maybe thousands, I don't know. A lot. And they were very eager to find Griese."

"They didn't do too good a job of it, considering he was lying naked in an alleyway."

"You're forgetting, nobody knew he was dead. They were searching for a man on the run, not a dead man. It's easy to overlook a body hidden under some garbage in a dark alleyway not far from where he had first disappeared."

Naumann eyed the door. Vogel's young partner would be returning at any moment. "What do we do now?"

Vogel sighed. "What would you normally do?"

"Me? I'd file some paperwork showing that I had his body here, and request Central Records confirm their report. I would assume they would then start an internal investigation, then eventually get back to me with their findings. In the past, on the rare occasion there has been some discrepancy, they never provide any details beyond whether they have confirmed they were right or I was right."

"And how often are you right?"

"Every single damned time."

Vogel chuckled. "Of course you are." He stood. "I suggest you do everything by the book. We never had this conversation. All we discussed was the report from Central Records, our confusion, and the fact you would report the possible error. The rest of the time, we discussed the weather while waiting for my partner to bring us a fresh carafe of coffee from your favorite café across the street."

As if on cue, the door opened, an upset Stadler entering carrying a hot carafe of coffee. Naumann rose.

"What took you so long?"

Stadler glared at him. "I thought you said they'd know you there."

"They didn't?"

"No, it was a new girl. She had never heard of you."

Naumann shrugged. "Hardly my fault now is it?" He pointed at several cups sitting on the table. "Pour, young man, pour!"

Stadler growled but poured, serving up the steaming cups in short order. He sat in Vogel's chair with a sigh. "So, what did I miss?"

"A lovely discussion about the weather."

Stadler eyed Naumann. "We had an urgent message for us to come here in order to discuss the weather?"

Vogel saved him. "No, the good doctor was informing us that he received a report from Central Records indicating our Corporal Griese had already been found dead last night from wounds suffered in the air raid."

Stadler nearly spilled his coffee. "What?"

"Obviously a clerical error," said Naumann. "I'll be sending in the paperwork to Central Records so they can figure out what went wrong."

Vogel sipped his coffee, walking over to the table holding Griese's body. "The good news is that we have confirmed this is indeed Corporal Griese."

Stadler shifted in his chair. "Not good news for him." He chewed his lip for a moment. "Wait. The colonel said he was cut by falling glass. This guy doesn't have any cuts."

"No, but he does have a bullet wound to the ear that the colonel might have mistaken for a cut."

Stadler's eyes narrowed. "But that means there was a second shooter."

"No, it means Griese wasn't the shooter at all. He was shot." Vogel drained his coffee then placed the empty cup in the sink. "Let's go, I'll bring you up to speed on the way back to the scene. We don't want to delay the Doc's report to Central Records."

Stadler scrambled to his feet, sipping his coffee all the way to the sink before rushing after his senior partner.

Leaving Naumann the unenviable task of pointing out to Central Records that they had made a mistake, knowing full well that they had actually been deceived.

I should have called in sick.

Friedrichshain People's Park

Berlin, Nazi Germany

Joachim sat up in the tree, a favorite hiding spot of his in the park near their new home. He had discovered it the first week they had been there while exploring with his brother. Their new home was large, far larger than their previous, and in a part of the city where he knew no one.

He had hated it.

But once he had realized how important his father's new position was, and how powerful he had become within the SS, the organization he once dreamed of serving in, perhaps for the great Himmler himself, he had softened to the idea of living here.

Yet he still found it hard to make friends.

The school year was just about to begin, but the Hitler Youth went strong all year round, especially during the summer, where he thrived. His was an elite unit, filled with the sons of senior officers, and he quickly learned he was nothing special, as his father was merely one of many colonels in the organization.

School would be a different story. There he might not be at the top in the hierarchy fathers brought, but he'd be close, and certainly far higher than most.

There he would gain the respect he deserved, and once he finished university, he'd be an officer, and with his father's rank and contacts, he'd work his way up quickly.

You have to volunteer for the front.

It was the quickest way for advancement. Prove your bravery, your capability, your willingness to serve and die for the Führer, and you'd soon find yourself a senior officer.

His stomach growled.

Yet none of that was possible now.

And who was he kidding? He was a coward.

He had shot that bastard corporal, yes, but he had done it with his eyes closed, tossing the gun moments after firing as he ran off into the night, sobbing.

Real soldiers don't cry.

He wasn't officer material.

He wasn't even corporal material.

He was nothing. A pathetic coward who had run away crying, rather than standing proudly over the body of the vanquished enemy that had dared embarrass his family.

He had found his perch quickly, losing whoever was pursuing him when the air raid had begun. Oddly, the thought of dying from bombs dropped by Allied aircraft overhead never bothered him. It would be a waste to die like that, though it never troubled him. His attitude might change if he actually saw any bomb damage, as where they lived hadn't suffered any as of yet. It angered him to no end that the Allies would dare bomb his city, the capital of the great Third Reich, and beating heart of what would soon be the greatest empire the world had ever known.

Yet it wouldn't be led by people like him, people who vomited at the mere thought of having killed a man, despite his guilt.

He groaned as his stomach rumbled again.

I'm starving.

The city was alive around him. People strolled through the park, some under the very tree that was now his hiding place, and the sounds of cars and trucks going about their business as if last night's events hadn't occurred had lulled him to sleep on more than one occasion.

What are you going to do?

He couldn't go home. Not with what he now knew. They were all traitors, liars, deceivers. If he were to go home, it would be to rescue his brother from the clutches of those who would call themselves loyal to their Führer.

Yet it was too dangerous.

He could only think of one thing to do. Report his deed to the SS. After all, it was one of theirs he had killed, and they should know exactly why he had done it, then report what he had discovered about his family. They deserved it for what they had done.

His stomach flipped as he pictured his mother, smiling, his brother giggling, and his father reviewing paperwork at his desk.

They'll all die.

Yet shouldn't they?

He gasped.

I'll die!

He shook his head, refusing to believe it. They don't kill for that. Not the children. His parents, possibly. His father would lose his position, certainly, though deservedly so. He had lied, he had hidden the truth. He couldn't be trusted with the position he had been granted.

Would they kill his mother?

They might. It was ultimately her fault, wasn't it?

He wasn't sure. Certainly his father played a part, did he not?

He sighed.

Why did I have to see that photo?

He closed his eyes. Life had been so much simpler yesterday, his future planned out, and now he was losing it all, all because of something that wasn't his fault.

He growled.

He had to reclaim his future.

He had to take responsibility for his actions, and hope that his actions would be praised by those superior to him, that he'd be given a second chance, perhaps adopted by another family that could be trusted to serve the Führer, with no secrets to hide, no lies to tell.

No love to give him.

His eyes burned, his heart ached, and he grabbed his knees, pulling them close to his chest.

What am I going to do?

"Hey, you there!"

He flinched, enough to lose his balance and fall from his perch, hitting several branches on the way down before coming to a painful halt as he was caught by the unforgiving ground.

A police officer in his green uniform towered over him. "Are you all right, boy?"

He groaned, not entirely sure.

Hands roamed his body and he winced a few times, though there were no yelps that might indicate something broken. He was hauled to his feet.

"What's your name?"

"Joachim."

"Joachim what?"

"Konrad."

"Konrad?" The officer's eyes narrowed and he pulled out his notebook, flipping through it. "Ahh, I thought so. You're the boy who ran away from home last night. Your parents are worried sick about you."

"They're not my parents. Not anymore."

"What the devil are you talking about?"

Joachim realized this wasn't the man to tell his secret to. He needed to talk to someone in the SS. He shoved his hands on his hips. "Take me to Reichsführer Himmler."

The officer tossed his head back, roaring with laughter. "Oh, sure, and after that, how about I take you to see the Führer!" He grabbed Joachim by the arm and led him from the park. "Before your meeting with Himmler, I think we'll make sure your parents approve."

Joachim tried to break free, but the grip was like iron. He finally saw no choice. "I killed someone."

And with those three words, everything changed.

Konrad Residence

Berlin, Nazi Germany

"Shouldn't we have heard something by now?"

Konrad frowned as he wiped the corners of his mouth with his napkin. "I would have thought so, but there were quite a few casualties last night, so it might take time."

"You should have gone to the morgue. You could have identified him already."

He shook his head. "I needed to stick to the story that he was cut by the glass, otherwise they might suspect Joachim in the shooting."

"I suppose." She looked at him. "Those policemen. Will they cause problems?"

He sighed, his soup forgotten as he leaned back and took in his wife's concerned expression at the other end of the table. He should never have told her what had happened, but she had badgered him until he finally gave in.

Then spent the rest of the morning worrying. He finally left for the office for a couple of hours, returning with the faint hope there might have been word about Joachim or Griese delivered here instead of at work.

Neither hope had been fulfilled.

"They might."

She dropped her spoon in the bowl, its contents splashing on her unnoticed. "Could we have made things worse?"

He frowned. "*I* might have."

"It was my idea."

"An excellent idea at the time, and one that I agreed with, and *I* executed."

She finally noticed the soup on her blouse and dabbed at it with her napkin. "What will happen?"

"Well, assuming the man at the morgue is Griese, and you and I both know it likely is, then Central Records will have been sent his fingerprints. They will eventually match them to his file, and note him as dead. More likely, they will have already noted he was dead, because the identity papers I took from his quarters and planted on the other man will have been used to identify him already. This discrepancy will be noticed by someone, and they will investigate. The police said the man they found had two gunshot wounds. That means murder, so this matter won't be dropped."

Renata returned her napkin to her lap. "Wouldn't they assume the murderer took the papers and placed them on another body? I mean, you were lucky to find his papers in his quarters, weren't you?"

He shrugged. "Not particularly. He was at his post, a private residence. There was really no need for him to have them on his person, and thank God for that." He frowned. "Though perhaps I shouldn't thank Him, since it looks like this might backfire on us."

"But in the end, it's the same result, isn't it? As soon as you have official word that he's dead, you can inform General Graf, and then we don't have to worry about him launching his own investigation. That was the entire point of this, wasn't it? To deal with his twenty-four-hour deadline?"

"Yes, though with the murder investigation, it could invite the same questions."

She scratched behind her ear then shifted in her chair. "What should we do?"

"We rid ourselves of any evidence." He stared at her. "*Any.*"

She paled. "You can't be—"

"Would you prefer death?"

Tears filled her eyes. "But it's all I have left."

His heart ached at her pain, and he rose then knelt beside her, taking her hands. "I know, my love, but we have no choice. We have to think of the children. Joachim is still out there, filled with rage and confusion, and Griese has been murdered, and the police are investigating. And my poorly thought out actions last night have just made things worse. We could have Graf's men and perhaps even the Gestapo swarming over this house at any moment. If they find anything, and I mean *any*thing, we're done for."

She sighed, finally acknowledging he was right. "I'll take care of it." Her shoulders shook. "I always knew this moment would come, though with each passing day we weren't found out, a small part of me thought it might not."

He patted her hand. "Let's take this one day at a time. Nobody knows I planted the papers on Griese, and everyone will assume he had them on his person, as the law requires. That means they'll think the murderer tried to deceive the police by planting them on someone else. This is the only logical conclusion they can make. That means there should be nothing to make them suspicious of us. If for some reason they do become suspicious and search the house, they'll find nothing. That will hopefully assuage any concerns, and they won't bother doing a deep dive into our records." He smiled. "If we make it through the next few days, we should be fine."

"You're forgetting one thing."

His eyes narrowed. "What's that?"

"Joachim."

Strausberger Straße

Berlin, Nazi Germany

"So, what did you find out?"

Sergeant Hellwig flipped open his notebook as Vogel and Stadler approached. "Well, it was a good thing we went back. Nobody agrees on whether there were two or three shots, but all agree there was more than one, and that at least one shot sounded different than the others. Certainly sounds like two different weapons, two different calibers."

Vogel smiled slightly, elbowing his partner. "See, footwork pays off sometimes." He turned back to Hellwig. "And did you have to beat this information out of anyone?"

Hellwig chuckled. "Not today."

Another elbow. "See?"

Stadler stepped out of reach. "Yeah, yeah. You made your point. But doesn't that just confuse things?"

"What do you mean?"

"I mean, if he was shot in the ear by a small-caliber weapon at the colonel's residence, then why was he shot at again with the same or similar weapon, then killed with a larger caliber weapon, all the way over here?"

Vogel frowned, his joy short-lived. The kid was right. It didn't make sense, though only if they assumed it was the same small-caliber weapon at both locations.

But if they weren't, it was one hell of a coincidence.

"We need a motive."

"The colonel didn't provide one? What was this incident he spoke of?"

"I'm still deciding if it's relevant." Vogel had made a promise to not divulge anything that wasn't necessary, and if he were to break that promise, it certainly wouldn't be with Stadler, in public, where word would spread like wildfire if the wrong person overheard. "Unfortunately, he provided no motive for the murder of our victim." His stomach was queasy. He hated lying, though this was technically an omission. A motive was never part of their discussion, nor, frankly, the murder.

The incident, however, did provide possibilities. If everyone had been operating under the assumption that Griese had taken a shot at the guests, then that in itself could be a motive.

Justice.

Yet if he were killed because of his criminal actions, then why hide the fact? Shoot him, drag his body back to the residence, and pronounce the incident resolved.

Though that wasn't the truth. Someone had tried to shoot Griese last night, at the residence. He was convinced of that. And whoever that someone was, had a motive for that initial shooting, a motive that could easily have carried over to the second shooting. And that was perhaps exactly what happened, since the witnesses reported hearing two different caliber weapons.

A thought occurred to him and he turned to Hellwig. "Did the witnesses indicate how much time elapsed between shots?"

Hellwig nodded. "They were almost on top of each other, maybe a second in between, perhaps two."

Vogel chewed his cheek, disappointed with the answer. If the shooter had pursued Griese, fired a warning shot, then disarmed the corporal, relieving him of his sidearm, he could have then shot the man with the higher caliber weapon. But that took time, and one or two seconds certainly wasn't enough.

There had to be two shooters.

There *had* to be.

"There has to be two shooters then."

He glanced at Stadler. "Agreed, but that's about all we know. We don't know who did it, why, or how. All we really know is when."

"We know he was shot."

"Yes, but that's only a partial answer to the how. Were there indeed two shooters, or just one with two weapons? Or perhaps the second shot was from Griese himself. He would have been carrying a sidearm."

Hellwig shook his head. "He'd have a nine millimeter, or something equivalent. Not a small-caliber weapon. Didn't you say before that he was shot in the back with something bigger? If his weapon fired, there would have had to have been a third weapon involved if he was shot fatally, and all the shots happened within a second or two."

Stadler's jaw dropped. "The third shot!"

Vogel sighed loudly. "This just keeps getting more complicated by the hour. If Griese got off a shot with his weapon, and he was shot with something similar, and at the same time a shot was fired by a small-caliber weapon, then there were two shooters exchanging gunfire with Griese, all within a couple of seconds of each other."

Hellwig scratched at his neck. "Wait. If this all went down within a couple of seconds, and he was shot in the back, then doesn't that suggest he was shot at by the small caliber weapon from the front, and someone behind him shot him with the bigger gun?"

Stadler jabbed the air with a finger. "That makes sense. And he's trained SS. Would he have missed?"

Vogel shook his head. "We don't know the range. If the person with the peashooter missed, then perhaps it was from a distance." He paused. "Unless…"

Stadler's eyes narrowed. "What?"

"What if they didn't miss?"

"What?"

"What if there's a third wound. Just a graze. It might have been mistaken as a rodent bite."

Hellwig grunted. "Damned rats. With rationing, I've never understood how they can still survive and thrive."

Vogel chuckled. "Good question." He stared down the alleyway where the body had been found. "You know, if Griese fired his weapon, he might have found his target. There could be someone out there who's wounded."

Stadler nodded. "Or another body."

Konrad Residence

Berlin, Nazi Germany

Renata poked at the flames, making certain every last scrap was consumed as her shoulders shook with shame and horror. It was sacrilege what she was doing, destroying such memories, destroying all that she believed in.

This was the last of her family, the last bit she had held on to for so long.

Yet Rudy was right. It was too dangerous to keep anything from her past, from their past.

No matter how much it hurt.

She pushed the scraps toward the center of the flame, constantly looking over her shoulder to make sure she was still alone, despite the fact she had locked the door. She should be doing this in their bedroom, but starting a fire there during the day might raise questions, and this was the lone fire already going in the house where she could be alone.

And it had taken far too long. The only thing saving her from discovery was that the entire staff was tiptoeing around her, not wanting to upset her any more than she already was with Joachim still missing.

She worked the edges, pushing another scrap toward the flames when she paused, her heart hammering.

What is that?

She scraped the piece toward her then gingerly reached in, snagging it with her fingers while wincing at the heat cast from the well-fed fire. She brushed the ash off the thick piece of detritus then gasped as the unmistakable silver stitching embroidered on the collar of a uniform was revealed.

An SS uniform.

Her mouth filled with bile as she tossed the scrap on the flame, backing away from the fire as her mind raced with the implications. There was no doubt what it was. It was a piece of the collar from an SS uniform, a piece that had survived the fire, someone obviously doing a poor job of burning it.

But whose uniform was it? Her husband had told her that the body they suspected was Griese had been found naked. That meant the uniform had to have ended up somewhere.

And if it ended up in this household, in this fireplace, then obviously it had been put here by someone in this house, where her family lived.

She rushed forward, confirming her own destruction of evidence was complete, then placed the screen back in front of the fire before standing and brushing off her knees. She unlocked the door and attempted, poorly, to control her retreat to her bedchambers. She closed the outer door, locking it behind her, then did the same with the inner door, curling up on the bed and hugging her pillow as she rocked back and forth, trying to make sense of her discovery.

Someone had stripped Griese naked, then brought the uniform back here to burn it. Part of her was forced to acknowledge that whoever it was had likely thought they were helping in some way, though how that might be she had no idea. Nothing made sense. Who would strip him naked? Why would anyone bring the uniform back here? Why would they have tried to hide who he was? Were they protecting her family? Did they have an ally they weren't aware of?

Did they know their secret?

She shuddered at the thought. She was surrounded by SS soldiers constantly, and all were killers. Except for her husband. He wasn't a killer. He couldn't be a killer. Yet he was a soldier, in the SS. She didn't know a single SS senior officer who wouldn't kill, or who hadn't killed. She just assumed her husband wasn't one of them, though perhaps she was naïve. Did the other wives feel the same as she did about their husbands? Were there women out there who would proudly declare that their husband had executed some Jews or trade unionists with their bare hands?

She avoided socializing with the other wives as much as possible, though it was hard, and growing harder with her husband's new position. Being in the same room with many of these women made her skin crawl, the elitist crowd spending much of their time boasting of their husband's accomplishments, whose dinner party they had been invited to, whose spouse had disappeared after some scandal.

Yet none, that she could recall, ever boasted of their husband's latest set of personally carried out executions.

Senior officers delegated.

If her husband killed people, it wasn't by his own hand, unless you counted the fact it wrote the signature on the orders that ultimately led to the deaths of others.

But to pull the trigger?

To intentionally kill another human being?

She couldn't see her husband doing such a thing, yet he would if it came down to saving their family. And it was all her fault. Griese was dead, yet she was the one who deserved to die, not him. It was all because of the secrets this family had been hiding for so long. Secrets that could turn her beloved husband into one of the coldblooded killers that surrounded her every day.

He'll sacrifice his humanity to save us all.

Berlin-Mitte Morgue

Hannoversche Straße, Berlin, Nazi Germany

Naumann pointed at Griese's left shoulder. "This might be what you're looking for."

Vogel leaned in, staring at the small scrape on their victim's shoulder. He shrugged. "I can't tell. It could just be a scratch from dragging the body for all we know."

Naumann shook his head. "No, if the body was dragged while he was naked, then there'd be lots more. I think he was dragged then stripped." He pointed at the small scratch, less than three centimeters long. "This abrasion was not made by vermin."

"Why'd you miss it the first time?"

Both Vogel and Naumann gave Stadler a look. "Because I wasn't looking for it. I had two bullet wounds, including the fatal one. He's covered in scores of bite marks. There was no need to examine each and every one."

Vogel patted him on the shoulder. "No need to explain yourself to my impudent colleague. You found it when we needed it found. You're certain it's from a gunshot?"

"Not at all. I said *might* be what you're looking for. There's just no way to know for sure, though where it is, the fact it's tapered at the front and rear, deeper in the middle, suggests something passed through the first few layers of skin. Now, that could indeed be some sort of scrape, but there should have been dirt in the wound." He shrugged. "All I can say for certain is that I've examined every square centimeter of him now, and this is the only wound that *might* fit what you're looking for."

Vogel sighed. "Fine. Anything that suggests the angle?"

"Not really. I'd say they were standing directly in front of each other."

"Range?"

"No clue."

Vogel frowned. "So, we may or may not have a third gunshot wound, that might have been fired at point-blank range, or from twenty meters away for all we know."

"If we had his uniform, I could tell you more. If it were damaged on the shoulder, we could at least confirm it happened before he was stripped, and perhaps confirm it was a gunshot if there were powder burns or a bullet hole."

"Well, they've been searching the area all night and day, and haven't found it. My guess is it's been burned, or was placed..." He smiled. "Our second body. Was the victim wearing a uniform?"

Naumann's eyes widened. "You don't think..."

"You never know. The uniform went somewhere. Maybe he found a body with the necessary facial wounds, put it in Griese's uniform and planted the papers."

"It's definitely possible. I'll check right away. If we're lucky, they haven't processed the body yet."

The door opened and a uniformed officer entered. "Good, I found you. Sergeant Hellwig wanted you to know that we picked up that boy you were looking for." The young man checked his notepad. "Joachim Konrad."

Vogel and Stadler exchanged excited glances. "Where is he?"

"At headquarters. Apparently, he's demanding to talk to Himmler himself. Claims he killed someone last night."

Vogel's eyes widened. "You're kidding me."

The officer shrugged. "I'm not, but maybe the kid is."

"Has his father been notified yet?"

"Not when I left. Apparently, he doesn't want to see his parents. He'll only talk to Himmler."

Vogel grabbed the phone, dialing headquarters, and was soon on the line with the desk sergeant. "You still have him?"

"I put him in an interrogation room with some food. The poor kid was starving."

"Has anyone spoken to him yet?"

"Yeah, but no one has gotten anything out of him."

"Has Himmler showed up?"

The sergeant roared with laughter. "I'm sure he's on his way."

"What about the parents?"

"I've sent word."

Vogel frowned. "If they get there before I do, stall them. Paperwork or something. I need to speak to him first."

"Are you joking? His father's an SS colonel, isn't he? They'll line me up and shoot me, then line me up and do it again if I don't let him see his son. If you want to talk to him, get your ass down here before he does. *Sir.*"

Vogel hung up, there no time to waste. He headed for the door then turned toward Naumann. "Let me know what you find with that uniform."

"Good luck with your interrogation. Just tread lightly, my friend. Parents, especially SS colonels, can be very protective of their children."

"That's what I'm afraid of."

Konrad Residence

Berlin, Nazi Germany

Konrad sat at his desk, his thumb absentmindedly drumming on the blotter. Things weren't going according to plan, though they rarely did when plans were rushed. In his desperation to have Griese "found" before General Graf's deadline, he had planted the identity papers on a victim from last night's air raids, and it had backfired horribly.

The real Griese had been found, and now there was a murder investigation, and no doubt a Central Records investigation. He wasn't worried about Griese's body leading back to him—where else could it lead? Griese was one of his staff. It was always leading back to him.

What had him concerned was that now people were pulling records, and they might pull those related to him and his family. He had done his best to hide the secrets his family held, but he was certain a keen investigator, a motivated individual hoping to advance in the Reich, could find something, some forgotten morsel that would demand more answers.

Answers he wasn't prepared to give.

We should have left when we had the chance.

It was a common refrain that echoed through his head more often these days, yet it was too late. Where could they go? And how? Mainland Europe was mostly conquered. The only places to go now would be Spain or Switzerland, and getting to those borders, especially with his wife and two boys, one of whom would be unwilling to go, would be impossible.

It was too late.

If they could just get through this crisis, they might buy themselves months or even years of breathing room. Perhaps in time the paranoia that dominated the Reich might ease and he might track down the remaining records scattered across the country.

Or they might lose the war.

All of these things were possible, however unlikely.

Yet to move on, to prevent Graf from investigating, he had to have proof Griese was dead, and now through his own actions, that word that German efficiency should have already delivered him was delayed.

There was a knock at the door.

"Enter."

Captain Hoffman opened the door and stepped up to his desk, stopping with a slam of the heel. Konrad didn't bother chastising him for such formalities within the confines of his own home. It would fall on deaf ears. Hoffman was loyal to the Reich, to the SS, and to his commander. A perfect, disciplined soldier, who took pride in every aspect of the life he had chosen. "Sir, as requested, I've had the car brought around."

"Thank you, Captain." Konrad checked his watch and frowned. The hours were wasting away as Graf's deadline approached. "No word on Griese?"

"Nothing."

"I'm growing impatient. According to those policemen, he was reported dead last night. General Graf wants him found otherwise he's going to launch his own investigation, and we've still got scores of men scouring the city for him. All of this is a waste of the Reich's resources. Call Central Records, find out what the hell is going on. Tell them I want a copy of his record showing he's deceased. Tell them it's for General Graf, and if they refuse…well, you know what to do."

A smirk crept up one side of Hoffman's mouth. "Yes, sir. You can count on me, sir."

Konrad rose from his desk and grabbed his hat. "My wife is resting. She is not to be disturbed. Make that call then let me know what you find out. If you have to go to Central Records personally, then do it. I want that damned file in my hands before dinner. This has gone on long enough."

"Yes, sir."

He paused, turning slightly toward Hoffman. "And Captain?"

"Yes, sir?"

"Run a check on my son. See if he's been reported…"

"I understand, sir."

Konrad left Hoffman to make the call, his heart heavy with the thought his son might be dead, then strode outside, his car waiting, the driver standing with the door open. He was about to climb in when Hoffman rushed down the steps.

"Colonel!"

Konrad turned toward his aide. "What is it?"

"I just received a call. They've found your son! The police have him at their headquarters."

Relief swept over him.

Then fear.

His son had been found, and he had to get to him before anyone had time to question him.

Kriminalpolizei Headquarters

Prinz-Albrecht Straße, Berlin, Nazi Germany

"Are his parents here?"

The desk sergeant gave Vogel a look. "Whose parents?"

Vogel glared at him "Joachim Konrad. The one we just spoke about."

"Oh, no, but Himmler's in with him now."

Stadler's face brightened. "Really?"

Vogel backhanded his partner in the chest. "No, you fool." He returned his attention to the cheeky sergeant. "What room?"

"Four."

Vogel passed through the door and strode rapidly toward the interrogation room, stopping to calm himself before opening the door. He looked at Stadler. "You keep your mouth shut the entire time, understood?"

Stadler frowned. "Yes."

"No facial expressions, no gasping, no jaw dropping, no nothing."

"I'll just stand in the corner and count the floor tiles."

"Good. And do it with a smile."

"Huh?"

"This is a kid. We want him to feel comfortable, not like he's in the room with the Gestapo."

"Right."

Vogel opened the door and stepped inside, sporting a smile. He was greeted by a grim-faced boy in a dirty Hitler Youth uniform, his cheeks tear-stained, his arms folded. "Hi there! You must be Joachim." He took a seat opposite the boy. "I'm Kriminalinspektor Vogel, but you can call me Wolfgang." He gestured toward Stadler, already in the corner, a creepy forced smile on his face. "And my friend here is Kriminalassistent Stadler. You don't need to know what to call him because we don't let him speak." He winked at Joachim. "Let's just you and I have a conversation."

The boy stole a glance at Stadler, then aimed his stare at his knees.

"Now, I'm here to take your preliminary report for Reichsführer Himmler. Once I have all the pertinent information, I can brief him, and if he feels it merits his time, he has assured me he'll speak to you personally."

Joachim's eyes widened. "Really? You spoke to Reichsführer Himmler?"

"Not ten minutes ago. He's very interested in what you have to say after the events of last night."

Joachim paled slightly. "He knows about that?"

"He knows very little. Most of us know very little. Once you tell us what happened, though, we'll know a lot more." Vogel pulled out his notepad and pencil. "Now, you told the officer that found you that you had killed someone. Who was that?"

Joachim frowned, his eyes darting between the two men and various objects in the room. "You're going to tell Reichsführer Himmler?"

"I'll be phoning him the moment I leave the room, and if he agrees, taking you to see him personally. Tell me everything now, as completely and truthfully as possible, and you could be in his office within the hour."

Joachim shifted in his chair, then leaned forward, shoving his elbows onto the table, his entire demeanor changing. "I killed that corporal. I think his name is Griese. He embarrassed my father at an important dinner party. Though that wasn't really why I did it. It's because he knows—knew—about..." He stopped speaking, his eyes widening slightly. He abruptly sat back in his chair, his arms once again folded, his eyes aimed at the door.

"He knew what?" prompted Vogel gently.

"Nothing."

Vogel decided it was best not to pry at details the boy wasn't willing to volunteer.

Yet.

"Fine, we can come back to that. Now, you said you killed him. How?"

Joachim stared at the light overhead. "I shot him."

"With what?"

"My mother's gun."

"How did you get it?"

"I found it in—" Again he hesitated. "I just found it."

"That's fine. What type of gun was it?"

He shrugged. "I don't know. Small. Not like my dad's Luger."

"Fine. So, you took your mother's gun and shot Corporal Griese. Where did you shoot him?"

"Out back. By the window where the dinner was."

"How many times?"

"Just the once."

"Where did you shoot him?"

"By the window. I already told you that."

"No, I mean in the chest, in the head?"

"Don't you know?"

Vogel smiled. "I need to hear it from you."

Joachim shrugged. "I-I guess the chest."

"You guess?"

The boy flushed. "Well, that's where I was aiming."

"But you don't know?"

He sighed then threw his arms in the air. "Fine! I had my eyes shut! Is that what you want to hear? I closed my eyes and shot like a coward then ran away."

Vogel smiled gently, trying to calm the boy. "It's fine, no one here is calling you a coward. In fact, you're very brave. Not a lot of boys your age would have the courage to even take the shot."

A slight smile appeared out of one corner of his mouth. "Really? You think so?"

"I know so. Where's the gun now?"

"I threw it away."

"Where?"

Joachim shrugged. "In the backyard. I mean, I think I dropped it almost right away."

Vogel exchanged a glance with Stadler. If the gun had been dropped in the backyard, then it should have been found by someone. The fact it hadn't been reported meant someone at the household was hiding that fact, forgot to mention it, or it was picked up and was indeed the small-caliber weapon they were seeking that had been fired later. He was leaning toward the latter. "Where did you go after you dropped the gun?"

"I ran toward the park. I heard somebody running after me, but the air raid had started and it was so dark, I don't know who it was. I ran to the park, climbed the tree, then sat there until that policeman found me."

"You didn't see or hear anything else?"

Another shrug. "Just the bombs."

"No gunshots?"

"Not that I remember."

"Any people out that shouldn't have been?"

"I don't think so."

Vogel looked at his notes. "So, you found your mother's gun, found Corporal Griese behind the house, closed your eyes and shot him, ran away, dropping the gun almost immediately, thought someone was following you, then climbed the tree until an hour ago."

"Yes."

"Now, why did you take the gun?"

"What?"

"Something must have angered you enough to get it. What was that?"

Joachim shifted in his chair. "He embarrassed my father."

"How?"

"I'm not sure. Something happened with General Graf. I think it involved his wife. I don't know. I just know that the general was very angry and said that he wanted Griese reassigned to the Eastern Front immediately."

Vogel's eyes widened. Whatever had happened must have been truly egregious for a punishment such as that, though he had heard of Graf, and he was notorious for overreacting. It was a brave man, or a foolish one, that interacted with him voluntarily.

Some said he put Himmler to shame in the revenge department.

"If he was being sent to the Eastern Front, wasn't that punishment enough? Why kill him?"

"He, umm, embarrassed my father a second time."

"How?"

"He threw up."

Vogel's eyebrows shot up. "Excuse me?"

"He puked, you know. Outside the window. My brother and I saw him throw up. My brother laughed and everyone heard him, so we were sent to our bedrooms. It was so embarrassing."

"So, that's why you decided to kill him?"

"This dinner was important to my father. This was the first one he had hosted since his promotion. Everything had to go perfectly. And I was supposed to be allowed to observe everything, but that idiot corporal threw up and my brother laughed and we both got in trouble. How is that fair? I did nothing wrong!"

"You murdered a man. You don't think that's wrong?"

Joachim fell silent for a moment. "Not if he deserved it."

"You think a man deserves to die because he embarrassed your father?"

Joachim shrugged.

"I don't think you do. I think you shot him for another reason. You said he knew something. What was it he knew that he deserved to die?"

Joachim stared at the floor.

"Was it something about you?"

No response.

"Your father?"

Joachim shifted in his chair.

"Your mother?"

Joachim erupted. "Leave me alone! You've heard enough! Take me to Himmler! I'll only tell the Reichsführer!"

Vogel remained calm, letting the tirade continue as the young man's emotions got the better of him. Whatever it was that Griese had known had something to do with his mother, and perhaps on the periphery his father, or more generally, his family.

But it was definitely related to his mother.

The boy calmed, or at least fell silent, his chest heaving under his folded arms, his face red for his efforts.

"I can only take you to Himmler if I have a full report. You know that. Now, what is it Corporal Griese knew? It was something about your mother, wasn't it?"

A glare was the only response.

"What secret could your mother possibly be hiding that is so terrible, you felt it necessary to kill a man?"

"Oh, you'd be surprised!" Joachim's eyes shot wide at his utterance, clearly shocked he had admitted to the fact there was indeed a secret, and that it involved his mother.

"Why don't you surprise me? Maybe it's not as bad as you think." Vogel paused, a thought occurring to him. "You just discovered the secret, didn't you?"

Joachim glared at him, saying nothing, but nodded with a huff.

"That's good. Reichsführer Himmler needs these details. So, I assume it was last night that you discovered this secret?"

Joachim said nothing, though a grunt of confirmation was uttered.

"Just before you shot the corporal?"

Another grunt.

Vogel suppressed a smile. "You discovered it when you retrieved the gun, didn't you?"

Joachim's eyes flared then his shoulders slumped. "Yes."

"And where did you find the gun?"

The boy's eyes filled with tears. "In my mother's vanity. In her bedroom."

"How did you know it was there?"

"I saw it once."

"So, last night, after Corporal Griese vomited and you were sent to your room, you decided to kill him, so you got your mother's gun and saw something you shouldn't have seen."

He nodded.

"Something in her vanity?"

Another nod.

"What was it?"

"A photograph." Tears poured down the young man's face and Vogel's heart ached for him. He was betraying his own mother, and Vogel felt like a heel for forcing him, but a man was dead, and this boy had nothing to do with it, yet this secret might have everything to do with it.

It was their first hint of a motive since the case had begun.

"And what was this photograph of?"

"I-I can't say."

"Why not?"

"I-I can only tell Himmler."

"Why? Is it really that bad?"

Joachim sniffed. "Yes."

"So, you want to tell Himmler because you want to get your mother in trouble?"

The boy's eyes shot wide, staring at him in horror for a moment before his chin dropped to his chest. "I-I…" His shoulders shook as he finally gave in to the conflicting emotions that must have been tormenting him since the discovery of whatever secret his mother was hiding.

Vogel reached across the table and put a comforting hand on the boy's arm. He flinched, pulling away. "Listen, I know this is hard. Maybe we shouldn't tell Himmler just yet. Maybe you should just tell me, and let me decide if he needs to know. Maybe he doesn't. Maybe your mother doesn't need to get in trouble."

"But—but it's wrong. I mean, every day we're told it's wrong. They've been lying to us forever."

"Who has been lying?"

"Mother and Father! Maximilian knew. He remembered! I don't know how that fool remembered when I forgot, but he did!"

Vogel kept the confusion off his face. "Maximilian. Is that your brother?"

Joachim nodded, wiping his tears on the back of his hands.

"What was it that he remembered?"

"Frida!"

The door burst open and Vogel spun in his chair, about to deliver a verbal tirade on whoever had interrupted them when he saw it was Colonel Konrad and a woman he assumed to be his wife.

"Joachim!"

The woman rushed forward and the boy jumped into her arms, sobbing hard as they both embraced each other.

"I'm sorry, Mother! I didn't mean to! I won't tell anyone! I swear, I won't tell anyone!"

Konrad turned on Vogel. "What the hell do you think you're doing?"

Vogel rose. "Interviewing a murder suspect."

"You and I both know he had nothing to do with it!"

"I do now, but before I started questioning him, he was a prime suspect."

Konrad turned to his wife. "Take him to the car. I'll be there in a minute."

Vogel held out a hand to block them. "One last thing." He put his hand on Joachim's shoulder. "Son, you need to know something."

"Wh-what?"

"You didn't kill Corporal Griese."

His eyes widened. "Wh-what?"

"You missed. You shot him in the ear."

His jaw dropped. "He's-he's alive?" Joachim stared at his mother. "But he knows about Frida!"

His mother paled and reached for the wall to steady herself. Konrad batted Vogel's hand off his son. "He's dead, son. Someone else killed him."

Joachim seemed relieved, then turned to Vogel. "Are-are you going to tell Himmler?"

Vogel glanced at Konrad, the shock on the man's face quickly wiped away. "Do you want me to?"

Joachim shook his head vigorously. "No. Please don't."

Vogel smiled. "Then I won't." He turned to Konrad. "Though I need to talk to your father first."

The Colonel's wife led her son from the room, and Vogel turned to Stadler. "Give us a minute, would you?"

Stadler looked none too pleased, a look he must be growing accustomed to, but left the room, closing the door behind him.

"I'll have your job for this."

Vogel sat on the edge of the table, his arms folded, as he regarded Konrad. "I think not, Colonel, not with what I've just heard."

Konrad shifted from one foot to the other. "And just what is it you think you know?"

"Your wife's secret."

Konrad paled slightly. "Perhaps you should come to the house where we can talk. Alone."

Vogel nodded. "I'll be there in two hours."

Konrad left the room and Stadler entered, closing the door, his eyes wide. "Holy mother of God! What the hell just happened?"

Vogel sighed, still coming down from what he had just done to that young man. Joachim would carry the scars of their conversation for some time, though during the process, whatever horrible secret he was hiding, was no longer something he wanted to share with Himmler.

Depending on what it was, how bad it was, how much against doctrine it went, it could still mean their deaths, for he feared it was indeed a horrifying secret. It was clear to him that Joachim was battling everything he had been taught by the system, drummed into him since he was born, a system that tolerated little that deviated from the norm and didn't celebrate the notion of a pure Aryan.

Whatever that was.

With the history of Europe so replete with one state conquering another over thousands of years, how could anyone be pure beyond perhaps the naked eye. What lay beneath the fair skin, blond hair, and blue eyes so prized by a man who had none of these attributes beyond the skin color he shared with an entire continent, was beyond him.

What had this photograph revealed that had Joachim so upset he was willing to kill to keep its secret? For that's what had happened. He had discovered the secret, and was so shocked by it, he was, for a short while, willing to sacrifice his entire family because it offended him so much. Yet he had also shot Corporal Griese because he too had known the secret. His internal conflict was so out of control, he was at once willing to kill to preserve the secret, and to tell Himmler himself the very same.

He regarded his partner. "I'm not sure what just happened, but I'll know more later. He's asked me to come to the house to discuss everything."

"When do we go?"

"*We* aren't going anywhere. He asked me to come alone."

Stadler groaned. "I'm getting sick of being left out all the time."

Vogel grunted. "Enjoy it while you can. Once you're in my position, you can't avoid anything."

"So, what do we do now?"

"I'm going to prepare my notes while everything is still fresh, then put together a list of questions. I want you to run the name Frida Konrad through Central Records. See if they come up with anything. Oh, and find out what the wife's maiden name is, and run that too with the given name Frida."

"Who do you think she is?"

Vogel shook his head. "I'm not sure. He said his younger brother remembered her, and he had forgotten. I'm guessing it's someone they both knew years ago. Perhaps a relation."

"But what secret could that possibly hold? I mean, it's just a person he saw in a photograph. What could that photograph possibly have shown?"

"I don't know, but it might not be what was in the photograph that has him so upset. It could be that the photograph triggered a memory of this Frida person, and who or what she represents is what has him so upset."

Stadler's eyes widened. "You don't think she's a Jew, do you?"

Vogel frowned. "I hope not for their sake."

"We have a duty to report our suspicions."

Vogel eyed him. "What suspicions? Everything we've been discussing is pure conjecture. I'm not going to condemn a family, possibly to death, just because you think someone in a photograph might be Jewish."

Stadler bristled. "Remember our oath and our duty, sir. We are required to report all Jews."

"And we will, *if* that's what's going on here. But I don't think that's what's going on here at all."

"Then what do you think is going on?"

"I don't know, but I hope to in the next couple of hours. Now, leave me alone and run those names."

Stadler left the room, fuming, and Vogel watched him storm down the hall.

If they are Jewish, with him as my partner, they're doomed.

Konrad Residence

Berlin, Nazi Germany

Hoffman was relieved to hear Joachim had been found safe, yet he had a duty to perform. The colonel and his wife had rushed out of the home a short while ago, and he had been given the runaround by Central Records, finally threatening to come down in person with a squad of men to perform the search himself.

The threat had worked, a supervisor beckoned by a terrified clerk.

"This is Zimmer. To whom am I speaking."

"This is Captain Hoffman, aide to Colonel Konrad. I need—"

"How dare you speak to one of my people like that! Konrad, you said? I want to speak to him right now!"

Hoffman bristled. Years ago, a voice such as this would have had his stomach churning with fear, yet today, after all he had seen and done? It didn't bother him one iota. Not with the SS embroidered on his collar, the *Totenkopf* skull and crossbones on his hat. "He's not available, however if you'd like, I can transfer you to his superior, who is eagerly awaiting the results of my query."

"You do that."

"Very well, please hold for General Graf. It may take some time." He paused. "Oh, and your name again was?"

"Umm, Graf, you say? Well, we wouldn't want to disturb him now, would we?"

The subdued voice had Hoffman smiling. "*I* wouldn't, but you're insisting. Please give me a few minutes, I'll try to get him."

"No, wait, I didn't realize this was for him. What is it you wanted?"

"I wanted the records confirming the death of a Corporal Klaus Griese last night."

"Yes, umm, I have those here. You see, there's some confusion as to what happened."

"What do you mean?"

"Well, we have two bodies identified as Corporal Griese. Obviously, there's been some mistake, and we've launched an internal investigation to determine what's going on. It shouldn't take more than a few days to—"

"I need those records now. Not tonight. Not tomorrow. And certainly not a few days from now."

"But we're not sure he's dead."

"You're telling me that you have two bodies identified as Corporal Griese, and you think you might have made *two* mistakes, not just one?"

Heavy, desperate bursts of static were the response. "Umm, no, definitely not. One mistake is rare, two is unheard of."

"Then one of the records is correct."

"Yes. I'm quite certain that one of them is."

"Good, then make copies of both of them, and I'll come by within the next hour to collect them."

"Of course, Captain. They'll be waiting for you."

Hoffman hung up the phone and leaned back in his chair.

I love my job.

Berlin-Mitte Morgue

Hannoversche Straße, Berlin, Nazi Germany

"Are you sure?"

"Yes. I'm looking at it right now."

Naumann smiled. "Have it sent over immediately."

"I'll have it put with the next shipment tomorrow morning."

"No. Send it now. Special messenger. This is important."

"It's a corporal. Who cares?"

Naumann's chest tightened. All human lives were important, whether corporal or general, civilian or military. This mentality of lives being discounted because of their position or perceived value to the Reich was a plague spreading throughout Germany. He treated every single person that crossed his autopsy table as equal. Yes, some might take priority over others if there was some question as to how they died—Corporal Griese being one of them—but in the end, they were always given the same respect and reverence. "When I see you on my table, I'll be sure to remember where you rank in society."

There was silence at the other end of the line. "You can be an asshole sometimes, you know that?"

Naumann shrugged. "Better to be called one than to actually be one. I want that uniform in my hands in the next hour." He hung up before the asshole could respond.

You have to control your temper.

When he had started his career, saying things like he just had carried little risk. But now, under National Socialism, insulting the wrong person could lead to imprisonment, torture, even death. The man he had just insulted had no power to do anything to him, but perhaps he had an uncle who had the ear of someone in the Gestapo or SS. Someone who could make his life a living hell.

You really *have to control your temper.*

If they ever came for him, he had decided long ago he'd kill himself. He'd seen enough tortured bodies to know he didn't want to go through anything like it, even if he came out the other end alive. That was why he always carried a small scalpel with him. One quick nick of a major artery, and he'd be dead in under a minute, and the latter half of that would be a sweet oblivion.

He sighed. He hated such thoughts. Detested them. Committing suicide was a cardinal sin, a waste of a life, and would leave his family desperate and destitute. He had extended family that would take them in, assuming whatever agency had come after him would leave them alone, yet in today's Germany, even family sometimes wasn't willing to take risks for one another if that other was targeted by the Reich.

His eyes burned at the thought of his wife and kids, on the streets, begging for food, freezing in a Berlin winter.

He shook his head, ridding himself of the thoughts.

Get it together.

He growled.

And keep that damned temper in check.

He picked up the phone again and dialed Vogel's office. The man had to know that he had just confirmed there had been a third shot. The left shoulder of the uniform on the "second" Griese was damaged exactly where he had hoped it would be. And it confirmed more than one thing. It confirmed that there had been a third shot, but it also confirmed that the uniform had been taken and put on the second body. Any search for it could now be called off.

Though all of this did little to identify who the multiple shooters were.

Yet that wasn't his job.

Thankfully.

Konrad Residence

Berlin, Nazi Germany

"Soup and a sandwich, and draw a warm bath."

The first servant visible bowed at Konrad's orders then rushed off to see to them as they entered the house, Joachim only slightly calmer than when they had found him at the police station. Renata guided him toward the drawing room, but Konrad intercepted them. "Our bedchambers." He lowered his voice. "No one can overhear our discussion."

Renata paled slightly, but nodded. They climbed the stairs and took refuge behind the double doors of their bedroom, Renata sitting the boy on the bed, then taking up position beside him, her arm around his shaking shoulders.

Konrad pulled a chair from the corner and sat in front of them, forcing a calm smile and hopefully a calmer voice. "Are you all right, son?"

Joachim nodded.

"Just hungry?"

Another nod.

"And a little stinky," smiled Renata, pinching the boy's cheek.

He squirmed.

"Now, that police officer will be here later, and we're going to get this all straightened out. But I think you need to know some things before he gets here."

"We-we're not pure!" he cried. "My life is over! I was supposed to join the SS! I was supposed to be a general!"

Konrad's heart ached at the hate mixed with the self-centered concerns of youth. "Do you remember your sister?"

Joachim sniffed, rubbing his nose. "A little. I didn't until I saw the photo."

"Her name was Frida," said Renata, her eyes red, tears already rolling down her cheeks. "And she loved you very much. She loved your brother very much."

"What was wrong with her?"

Renata's shoulders shook and she buried her face in her hands. Konrad leaned forward, placing a hand on her leg, taking over.

"She was special. She had something called Down Syndrome. It's a defect that caused her to develop slower than normal children, and to appear different. But she was every bit our daughter, and every bit your sister."

Joachim stared at him. "Wh-what happened to her?"

"She died. With the eugenics movement, we knew she would never be accepted, so we kept her hidden. One day she ran outside and was hit by a car. I was at work, but your mother was there. There was no saving her. We buried her in secret, then mourned in private. We told you and your brother that we had sent her away so you wouldn't be traumatized by her death. You were about ten at the time. Frankly, I'm surprised your brother's the one who remembered her and not you."

"I-I forgot about her. When I saw the photo, I remembered. I remembered everything. What are we going to do? If they find out, we're finished!"

"Nobody knows except for the three of us. As far as the world is concerned, Frida was born and died. There's no record indicating she was mentally handicapped in any way. That photo has been destroyed"— he gave Renata a look and she nodded—"and as long as we keep the secret, no one will know."

"But the police officer. He knows. I told him!"

Konrad shook his head. "He knows nothing beyond a name. And lots of people have lost a child. We'll answer his questions, leave out that one tiny detail, then he'll leave. Everything will be forgotten, and life will go on as it did before."

"What if Griese told someone?"

"If he had, I'm sure we would have heard something by now. Besides, there was no time. He died shortly after he ran away, if what the police tell me is true."

Joachim's shoulders sagged. "But it still means we're not pure. We had a freak for a sister."

Renata slapped his hands. "You will never refer to your sister like that. She was the sweetest of souls, and would be heartbroken if she ever knew you thought of her like that."

Joachim shriveled. "Sorry, Mother."

Konrad leaned closer. "Now, you and your brother are perfectly good German boys, perfectly Aryan like the Reich desires. Your sister in no way diminished this family, nor you or your brother. All your future plans can still happen as long as no one ever knows about Frida and why she was special. Understood?"

"Yes, Father."

"Good. Now, I suggest we never mention her again, as it will raise questions. Let's just remember her in our thoughts. It's especially important for your brother to not know any of this. He's too young."

"But he's talking to her all the time."

"He's talking to an imaginary friend. All he likely remembers is the name. If anyone were to ask, he'd tell them she's real, and they'd know immediately it was all in his head, just the overactive imagination of a boy. He'll grow out of it eventually."

"Will you ever tell him the truth?"

"Perhaps, one day, when the Reich permits people like her to live. But with *Aktion* T4 official policy right now, I don't know when that might be."

His stomach churned at the thought of the brutal policy signed by the Führer two years ago. Tens of thousands had been "humanely" euthanized, the excuse given that death was more compassionate than forcing them to live handicapped, whether mentally or physically. Every time he drove past #4 Tiergarten Street, where the name Aktion T4 came from, he was forced to relive the death of his precious Frida, and dwell on the thoughts of how today, with his rank and stature, if she were alive, there would have been no way to hide her.

They would have taken her away, killed her, and stripped him of his rank and status.

Though he'd have died in the process, for there would have been no way she'd be taken without a fight.

It was always the ultimate solution to their problem. He had the cyanide capsules locked in his desk at home. If they came for them, Renata knew where they were. Whoever got there first would distribute them to the boys then each other.

They couldn't be taken. Though his wife and the boys were innocent, they would be used against him, tortured in front of him until he told them whatever they wanted to hear.

And he could never let that happen.

A knock on the outer door snapped him from his train of thought.

"Yes?"

"I have Master Joachim's lunch. Where would you like it served?"

Konrad walked over to the door and opened it, taking the tray. "He'll have it here. And the bath?"

"Drawn down the hall."

"Very well. I'm expecting a guest in about an hour. When he arrives, have him shown to the drawing room then let me know."

"Yes, sir."

He closed the door and brought the tray in, placing it on the vanity that had been the holder of so many secrets. Joachim leaped to his feet and grabbed the sandwich and glass of milk, devouring it in short order, the travails of the past day forgotten at least momentarily. Konrad sat beside his wife and squeezed her hand as they watched him. He felt confident that Joachim would keep their secret, especially if he could keep him away from the detective.

And keep Graf off their backs.

He sighed, putting an arm around Renata's shoulders.

We might yet get through this.

En route to Konrad Residence

Berlin, Nazi Germany

Vogel drove in silence toward Colonel Konrad's residence. Quite often when alone, he talked to himself, much to his own annoyance, especially when caught by someone in the next car, or on the crosswalk.

But today his thoughts were his own.

He was about to get questions answered, yet he had a suspicion they wouldn't be the ones he needed.

The uniform had been accounted for. Naumann had called to let him know it had been received and confirmed to be Corporal Griese's. He had called off the search, and the canvassing of the area was finished. They had learned all they would from the neighbors, which had proved fruitful.

There were definitely two shots, and still possibly three, by at least two different types of weapon.

Naumann had reported small entry and exit holes in the uniform he felt could be caused by the .22 caliber weapon, but not the 9mm they had confirmed delivered the fatal shot. And with Joachim having tossed his mother's gun, it was likely that somebody had picked it up then shot at Griese a second time.

Though they only had Joachim's word on that. He could have been lying about dropping it.

"No, he was telling the truth."

His voice startled him and he chuckled.

He was tense. He was treading on dangerous ground. This case involved the SS, and even though he was technically SS, the *true* SS didn't think so.

They were fanatics.

He was a cop.

He would hopefully soon know who Frida was, and why she was so dangerous to the Konrad family. He would know why Joachim had done what he had. Yet unless there was some miracle confession, some slip-up on the colonel's part, he wouldn't be leaving the Konrads' house with any more idea of who the murderer was.

Though he might be leaving with the motive.

And motive could allow him to narrow the suspect pool considerably, for those with no concern for the motive were unlikely to murder.

Yet he kept coming back to the fact there were two shooters at the murder scene. One likely standing in front of Griese, one behind him. Who were they? Why two of them? Why did they shoot from opposite directions? Why at almost the same time? Did Griese shoot back? Did he hit the shooter in front of him? Did they both strip him? Did they both dress another body in his uniform and plant his ID?

There were so many unanswered questions, it was frustrating.

Though it hadn't even been 24 hours.

He'd wrapped up cases in less time, though it was rare. It usually depended on whether it was well planned or hastily executed. The latter meant mistakes, meant clues left behind, meant a big red flag indicating those responsible.

And he had a feeling that whatever happened last night, wasn't planned at all. If it had been, Griese would never have been given the chance to run away. They wouldn't have had to strip him and have another body identified as him.

That was another thing that had him puzzled. Why had they done this? Why not just let the body be discovered in its own time? The only theory he had come up with was a time constraint. The murderer couldn't direct anybody to the corpse, otherwise he would become a suspect. That was understandable. But to dress a corpse and plant the ID, knowing that the body would eventually be found regardless, and that this discovery would pose questions, had to mean a hastily executed impulse borne of necessity.

"They needed the record to show he was dead."

He smiled.

"The *official* record."

If the official record showed Griese was dead, then the search would be called off, and any further investigation might be halted or at least stalled. The murderer must have felt that there was no way to tie any of it back to him, so he didn't care if there were two bodies later identified as the corporal. He didn't care if there was confusion at Central Records.

All they cared about was the deadline.

A smile crept up the side of his cheek.

Even though he didn't necessarily have a motive yet for the murder, he might find out who had a motive for wanting Griese's death to be discovered. Who would benefit from the search being called off? Who would benefit from having the spotlight taken off them?

Konrad?

It was the only thing that made sense. He would be the one under pressure to find the man thought to have taken a shot at his dinner guests. The colonel had said there were people there that outranked him. They were likely all SS, and that meant egomaniacs. They would demand Griese be brought to their form of justice immediately. And if he couldn't be found, Konrad would be the next on the chopping block as not only his commanding officer, but the host of the gathering who had failed to provide sufficient security.

Yet it didn't make sense. Why would he bother hiding the fact he had killed Griese? Everyone thought Griese had shot at the party guests then fled the scene. If Konrad had found him and shot him, then nobody would have said anything.

And again, he kept coming back to how narrow the timeframe. He had little doubt this death wasn't premeditated, which meant whoever was responsible, was probably panicked and that meant mistakes.

He pulled into the driveway of the Konrad residence and a shiver ran up his spine as he saw the heavy SS presence.

He was walking into the wolf's den, and if he wasn't careful, he might end up just like Griese.

Konrad Residence

Berlin, Nazi Germany

Konrad watched as the detective's car came to a halt in front of the steps leading into the house. He turned to his wife, sitting on the edge of the bed, trembling.

"What if he wants to talk to me?"

"I'll say no."

"But he's the police."

"And I'm a colonel in the SS."

She smiled weakly. "That might work today, but it won't tomorrow. Eventually he'll get his way."

He placed a hand on her shoulder. "You're worrying about things that haven't happened yet." He paused. "Does anybody know you went out searching for Joachim?"

She stared at her hands, yanking at the handkerchief they gripped. "I-I don't think so, but I can't be certain."

"Then it's best we don't lie. I'll say that you went out briefly to search for him, then decided it was fruitless and returned home where you waited for me outside."

"If you think that's wise."

"I do. We can't lie to this man. He's trained to pick up on these things. I'll tell him the truth as best I can, then try and avoid anything that might be…uncomfortable."

She stared up at him, her eyes red. "What are you going to tell him about Frida?"

His stomach churned at the mention of her name. "As little as possible." He sighed. "If that is at all possible. If he thinks I'm being too evasive, he might think there's a motive for us to have killed Griese, and he might keep digging."

There was a knock at the outer door. "Kriminalinspektor Vogel is here to see you, sir," called one of his staff members, his aide not home when they returned, presumably at Central Records to retrieve the documents they needed to keep General Graf off their backs.

"I'll be there in a moment!" he called, then took his wife's hand. "This is it. I don't know how long it will be, but stay in here, and don't answer the door for anyone but me."

"What about Joachim?"

"Let him rest. When I checked on him, he was still sound asleep. I've left a note for him to come see you here should he wake up. It's essential Vogel doesn't speak to him again. He might break." He pulled in a deep breath. "It's time."

He headed downstairs and into the drawing room to find Vogel sitting in the same chair as earlier. He rose, extending a hand. "Colonel, good to see you again."

"Likewise. Can I offer you anything?"

Vogel shook his head. "No thank you, I'm fine." They both sat and Vogel positioned his notepad on his knee, his pencil ready. "First, let me apologize for upsetting your son earlier. I'm afraid in a murder investigation, these things can become necessary. I'm just happy that we found him alive and well, and that he had little to do with the events of last night. Things could have been much worse."

Konrad conceded the point, though wasn't convinced of it. Perhaps Vogel knew more than he did, and this might be more of a two-way street of information. "We're just happy he's safe."

"Good, good. Now, let's get the elephant out of the room, shall we? Who is Frida?"

Konrad's mouth watered and he shifted in his chair, having rehearsed the answer to this question repeatedly over the past two hours. "She's our daughter."

Vogel's eyes rose. "Your daughter? Is she here?"

Konrad sighed. "Our *late* daughter. She passed away almost six years ago. Car accident."

"I'm so sorry. I have two children myself, and can't imagine what it would be like to lose one of them."

"It is difficult."

"Your son said he saw a photograph in your wife's vanity. I suppose Frida was in that picture. Why would it trigger such a reaction in him?"

"I suppose because he had forgotten about her. In order to help them with the grieving process, we chose, in retrospect unwisely, to tell them she had gone away, then never mentioned her again. In time, Joachim must have forgotten her, and Maximilian was too young to remember much beyond the name."

"Yes, Joachim mentioned his younger brother remembered."

Konrad shook his head. "All he remembered was the name. He has an imaginary friend that he talks to, and he gave her the same name."

Vogel chuckled. "Children and their imaginations. My mother insists I had an imaginary friend named Karl. I have no recollection of that, however, why should I doubt my own mother?" He returned to his notes. "Can I see this photograph?"

Konrad's stomach flipped. "I'm afraid not. In an overabundance of caution to prevent a recurrence, I ordered my wife to burn the photo."

Vogel frowned. "That's unfortunate, and I would think unnecessary."

"Unfortunately, the existence of Frida could become an issue. With my position, some might question why we kept her hidden. It could lead to suspicions that aren't, well, to be risked these days."

Vogel regarded him, not saying anything, and Konrad had a sense the detective didn't believe him. Sweat trickled down Konrad's back, and he prayed his face remained dry. "Your son said Corporal Griese knew the secret as well."

Konrad nodded. "Apparently, he walked in on my wife sitting at her vanity, looking at the photo. He couldn't have known her name or who exactly she was, though it was a family portrait, so he must have surmised."

"Did he say anything?"

"No. In fact, he only made it to the inner doorway before he immediately left the room without saying anything. I'm not sure he ever knew my wife had spotted him."

"Why do you think Joachim would have wanted to kill him for knowing?"

"It would have been unfortunate for my corporal to know our family secret, though really little harm would have come of it as it's no crime to be private in these matters unless directly asked. I would have merely told Griese to please respect our privacy, and in fact, I had told my aide to have Griese report to my office after the close of the party."

Vogel's eyes narrowed. "Really? I thought the meeting was to have him transferred to the Eastern Front."

Konrad's heart hammered. How much had Joachim told this man? How much did Joachim actually know? He was already regretting having let the children participate last night, but now he was convinced it had been a terrible idea that would never be repeated if they made it out of this. "The meeting had two purposes, yes."

"What exactly did Corporal Griese do to merit such punishment?"

Konrad chewed his cheek for a moment, choosing his words very carefully. "He embarrassed one of our guests. An important guest."

"How?"

"He neglected to pay attention to the length of a young lady's dress, and allowed her escort to exit his vehicle early. The man stepped on the dress, causing a bit of a scene."

"Seems rather trivial, don't you think?"

Konrad nodded slightly. "I'm afraid this is not for me to say."

"And just who was this guest?"

"I'm afraid I don't remember the young lady's name."

Vogel smiled slightly at his useless dodge. "I mean her escort."

"I'm afraid the guest list is classified."

Vogel leaned back in his chair, his pencil tapping on his pad. "I can run this up the chain of command and get the complete list, as you well know. And in a murder investigation, I have that right, and likely that necessity. You and I both know that it was General Graf, so why not just admit it?"

"You appear to be very well informed."

"I make it my business to know as much as is humanly possible. So, General Graf was embarrassed, ordered you to have him sent to the Eastern Front, then this same man is accused of taking a shot at the dinner party. I'm assuming the general thought the shot was meant for him?"

Konrad frowned. "He didn't say, though I think your assumption is reasonable."

"And then Griese ends up dead shortly after that."

"Yes."

"Do you know who killed him?"

"No."

"Do you think the general might have?"

Konrad's heart hammered with the idea. Could he direct the suspicion toward the general? If he could, there was no way any police detective would dare continue the investigation. It would be suicide. Yet he had to be careful. "The general couldn't have personally done it, no. He was in the bomb shelter with the rest of the guests."

"Are you certain?"

"Yes."

"Could one of his men?"

Konrad made a show of slowly bobbing his head and staring into the distance as if deep in thought. "I suppose that's possible. There was a special contingent of half a dozen men here because of him. I suppose he could have sent them out to find Griese with orders to shoot him." He tossed some doubt in there for good measure. "But didn't you say Griese was found naked? Why would the general do that? I mean, he wouldn't need to have the shooting covered up." He let his jaw sag slightly. "Ahh, maybe he wanted to humiliate him?"

Vogel didn't appear to be taking the bait. "Then why the second body with Griese's identity papers and uniform?"

Konrad gripped the arms of his chair tightly, his knuckles turning white. Vogel's eyes fixed on them momentarily and he forced himself to relax. This was quickly falling apart. He felt as if every answer he gave was being picked apart by this detective, a man old enough to obviously have a lot of experience in dealing with the criminal element. If things kept going the way they were, they were all at risk.

He had to do something.

And he could think of only one thing.

"Detective, can I speak to you father to father?"

Vogel regarded him for a moment then nodded, flipping his notebook shut. "Of course."

Konrad rose and retrieved his wallet. He reached into a hidden fold and pulled out a small photo. He closed his eyes for a moment, the tears burning, then handed the photo to Vogel. Vogel's eyes widened and he fell back in his chair.

"This is Frida?"

"Yes."

"This is your family's secret?"

"Yes."

Vogel handed the photo back and Konrad returned it to its hiding place. "I can see why you wanted no one to know. What do they call that condition?"

"Down Syndrome."

"And with Aktion T4 in place, now would be a terrible time for such a discovery to be made."

"Exactly." Konrad sat back down, his heart pounding, though the weight on his shoulders slightly lighter. "She did die six years ago in a car accident. Nothing of what I told you is a lie. But now you know why we had to keep it a secret. Now you know why Joachim was so upset when he saw the photo. He realized the implications. If Command were to discover we had a mentally handicapped child, I would be blacklisted. I'd lose my position, my career, and my son, who has dreams of being an SS general some day, would have no hope of being anything of value in the Reich. His entire future was crumbling around him last night. He had already been embarrassed, and evidently blamed Griese. He retrieved the gun to seek his own childish justice when he saw the photo. Then his future truly collapsed. Somehow, he must have found out Griese knew, shot at him, then ran away."

"Apparently Griese told him that he knew the secret."

"Then that settles it. And it's what I feared as I began to piece things together last night. My wife told me that Griese had caught her looking at the photo, we discovered the gun missing along with our son's Hitler Youth dagger on the floor, so we knew he had seen the photo as well. I went out in search of my son and…"

Vogel leaned forward. "And?"

"This, sir, is where I must ask you to listen to what I have to say with the ear of a father."

"Of course."

"I found Griese. Dead. Shot in the back."

Vogel's eyes widened. "You found the body? Was he stripped?"

Konrad shook his head. "This is where I'm ashamed to admit I panicked. I assumed my son had shot him. I was terrified that if the authorities found out, that questions would be asked, and with my son's state of mind, the truth about Frida might be revealed, and we would be ruined. In my panic, I dragged the body into an alleyway and buried him under a bunch of trash. I returned home to see if Joachim had come back and he hadn't. Troops were arriving en masse to begin a search, and I knew they might find the body and Joachim might be accused. I took my car, stripped Griese of his clothing and ID, then headed toward where the bombing had occurred. Fortunately, I quickly came upon an area close by where an enemy bomber had crashed into a house. I found a body inside the building badly maimed. There was no one around, so I put him in Griese's uniform, burned the photo off his ID, then planted it on him. I returned home, no one the wiser."

Vogel's head slowly shook in disbelief. "But why?"

Konrad tensed. "What?"

"Why go to all the trouble?"

"To protect my son."

"How does that protect your son?"

The world closed in on Konrad as he debated what to say. "I was on a deadline."

Vogel's eyebrows shot up. "A deadline?"

"General Graf gave me twenty-four hours to find Griese. I couldn't exactly tell everyone where he was, because I wasn't supposed to know, and I believed my son had shot him. By planting the papers at a site damaged in the air raid, I knew he'd be identified and reported very quickly so I could satisfy the general. As well, by making it look like he had been murdered some distance away, it meant Joachim couldn't be the killer so he wouldn't be questioned."

"And when the real Griese was discovered?"

"I had hoped Joachim would be home by then, and we'd have had a chance to calm him down and explain to him about Frida. With Griese dead, and Joachim calmed, no one would know our secret, and certainly no one would suspect our involvement with the deception, so life would go on with a mystery that might never be solved."

Vogel pursed his lips, staring uncomfortably at Konrad. "You know, this causes me problems."

Konrad nodded. "I'm aware. I just hope you realize that I did what I did to protect my son, as any father would."

Vogel drummed his fingers on the arm of his chair. "Yes, I see that, and while I might not have done the same, I can't declare unequivocally that I wouldn't."

"So, what do we do now? Do you have to report this?"

"So many problems." Vogel sighed. "If I report that you did this, your career is over."

"Agreed."

"And questions will be asked as to why you did it. Those will inevitably lead back to Joachim. He will be questioned, alone, and will likely be told that if he cooperates and tells them the truth, he will continue on to the glorious future he has planned for himself, and may even be told the same will be true for you. In his youthful exuberance, he will reveal the secret of Frida, and both your careers will be ended."

"Unfortunately, that's exactly how I see this playing out as well."

Vogel eyed him. "You took an awful chance telling me this."

"I sense you are an honorable man."

Air exploded from Vogel's mouth as he sat forward. "Unfortunately, my partner isn't, and he heard every word Joachim said earlier. He's going to demand answers."

"And what will you tell him?"

Vogel intertwined his fingers in front of him, staring at the floor for a moment. "The truth. A partial truth. Frida demands an explanation. Your initial one was good. She was your daughter who died six years ago in a car accident. To protect the boys from the trauma, you told them she went away, and then never mentioned her again. Last night, in a fit of rage at being embarrassed, Joachim went to retrieve the gun he knew his mother kept in her vanity so he could punish Corporal Griese. He found the photo, his memories came back, and when Griese admitted he too knew the secret, Joachim shot him in a fit of rage."

Konrad raised a finger. "Umm, is there any way to keep that out of the official record? General Graf probably won't take too kindly to having been shot at, however indirectly, by my son."

"Unfortunately, my partner knows this part of the story, and we have to be very careful to make certain there's nothing that contradicts what he knows. General Graf will hopefully forgive you."

Konrad grunted. "That's unlikely, though I fear his opinion of me is pretty low right now, regardless."

"Well, hopefully we can have your involvement in this sorted in short order and he'll lose interest. So, your son shoots, hits Griese in the ear, then runs off into the dark, dropping the gun in your yard in the process. You go out to find him, return unsuccessful, then take your car out to cover more territory before returning to coordinate the efforts to find Griese and your son from your residence. Am I missing anything?"

Konrad was filled with hope, his chest swelling at what this stranger was willing to do for him and his family. It renewed his faith that there was a greater Germany that was inherently good, despite so many having been taken in by the madmen now in charge. "Not that I can think of."

"Then that is our story."

Konrad hesitated to ask the question that demanded asking. "What about the murder investigation? Where do you stand on that?"

"Well, a few questions have been answered that I no longer have to try and run down, though I'm not much closer to finding out why he was shot in the first place. Assuming, of course, that what you're telling me is the truth."

Konrad tensed. "I assure you, every word is true."

Vogel smiled slightly. "And every guilty man would say the same. For the moment, however, let's go under the assumption you are indeed telling the truth. I do have some additional questions for you."

"Of course."

"Your son says he fired the gun then turned and ran, dropping it almost immediately. That means it should be in the backyard, but it wasn't. Who could have picked it up?"

Konrad shook his head. "I'm not sure. Griese?"

"That's a possibility, but I know he was shot in the shoulder, just a graze, by a small-caliber weapon. We're assuming it was that gun."

"Any number of people could have found it, I suppose. I was out there briefly, I think my aide Captain Hoffman was, probably all of the guards at one point." He shrugged. "Anybody, really." His eyes narrowed. "Are you sure it was the same weapon? Could it have just been a coincidence?"

"Possibly, though it would be one hell of a coincidence, don't you think?"

Konrad grunted. "I'm not familiar with the business of murder, sir, so I will bow to your superior knowledge on the subject. Did you have any other questions?"

"Yes, where was your wife during all of this?"

Konrad's heart hammered. "You suspect her?"

"Just routine."

"I must confess, she did go out in search of Joachim very briefly, but wisely returned after only a few minutes. In fact, she was waiting at the gate for me when I returned the first time."

"Did anyone see her?"

"I'm not sure. I would assume someone saw her leave the premises, though there was an air raid underway, so perhaps not."

"I assume your wife knows how to fire her own weapon?"

Konrad wasn't certain how to answer. If he told the truth, it could implicate her, but if he lied, and the truth was later found out, she might come under the microscope, something they couldn't afford. A thought occurred to him. "Yes. She's quite the shot, actually. She used to compete in her youth. I can assure you, if she shot at Griese with that weapon, there was no way she'd graze his shoulder. She'd have hit him dead center."

Vogel smiled. "We should put her on the front. Perhaps she could teach our boys a thing or two."

He chuckled. "She could end the war in two weeks."

Vogel flipped his notebook shut and rose, extending his hand. "I think we're done for now. I'll probably need to talk to you again, perhaps to your wife and staff. I'll try to keep Joachim out of this as much as possible. I'm going to go now and write up my official report as we discussed."

"Your discretion is appreciated."

Vogel smiled. "I'm a father too." He headed for the door then stopped. "Oh, I almost forgot. Classified or not, I'm going to need a list of all your guests, including their escorts, as well as any personnel, staff, chauffeurs and whatnot that were here last night."

Konrad frowned. "Is that necessary?"

"I'm afraid it is."

"Very well. I'll have my aide put the list together. He's not here right now, so it might be later in the day."

"Good. The sooner I get the list, the sooner we can figure out who did this, and you and your family can put this behind you."

Vogel bowed his head then left, leaving Konrad partly relieved at what had just happened, and equally nervous about providing the list. If the police began questioning his guests, especially the likes of General Graf, the end result they had just avoided might be worse.

We're not out of this yet.

Kriminalpolizei Headquarters

Prinz-Albrecht Straße, Berlin, Nazi Germany

Stadler stared at a map of the city, several pins stuck in it marking the Konrad residence, where the two different bodies had been discovered, and where the boy Joachim had been found. They had now confirmed that Griese's uniform had been on the second body. That could only mean that whoever had killed him had also dressed the bombing victim in his clothes. The distance was at least several kilometers between the two bodies, a distance that couldn't have been covered in the timeframe in question.

At least not on foot.

It meant someone with a vehicle had done it, and that narrowed the suspect pool down dramatically, for there weren't many civilian vehicles anymore, not with the war. And those would be few and far between at night, just after an air raid.

Then there was the fact Griese was likely killed by someone at the party or the Konrad residence. His money had been on the son, Joachim, but once he had checked the distances, he realized there was no way a boy, on foot, could have murdered Griese, stripped him, taken the uniform kilometers away, found another victim, dressed him, then returned to hide in a tree in a park near his home.

It was impossible.

That ruled the boy out.

His money was now on the father, Colonel Konrad. Konrad would have a vehicle, his rank would give him free access anywhere in the city, and Joachim had said there was some secret surrounding a girl named Frida, and when confronted, Konrad had insisted on meeting Vogel alone.

Which angered him to no end.

How the hell was he supposed to learn how to do his job if he kept being excluded? And he didn't trust Vogel. The man seemed more concerned with doing what was right according to the old code, rather than what was best for the Reich. His ways of thinking were out of date, and had no place in Hitler's Germany.

In fact, he was so concerned, he was keeping a file. At home. He wouldn't dare keep it here at the office in case someone stumbled upon it. So far, he didn't have anything damning enough to report to his superiors, but one day he was convinced he would, and with every other little thing the man had done that was suspicious or contrary to the new norm documented, it would all add up to enough to have the man's career ended.

He glanced at his partner's desk, a picture of his wife and children perched on the corner. If Vogel lost his job, they'd be destroyed. But that wasn't his problem as a loyal citizen of the Third Reich. That was Vogel's fault for not embracing the new ways as most had. He wasn't naïve enough to think everyone agreed with the way things were now run, but he was certain it was the vast majority, and with each new victory, those few slow to the fold were coming around.

And those that remained unconvinced? They'd be found out by the Gestapo.

And people like him.

He stared at the map. If Colonel Konrad was indeed involved, it could prove problematic. It all depended on how well connected the man was, and how far those connections would go to protect him. If they accused him of murdering Griese, and the ranks closed in to protect the colonel, it could mean a visit from the Gestapo for him and Vogel.

And those never ended well.

His career would be over before it started, and his life might even be at risk.

He sighed. No matter how convinced he was that Konrad had to be involved, he couldn't voice it. It was simply too risky.

Yet he was dying to hear what Vogel had found out.

He just wondered if he'd be told the truth by the man.

Vogel entered the room, greetings exchanged with some of the older men, then a coffee poured before he dropped into his chair. He nodded at the map. "What have you got there?"

"Just working on a theory."

"What's that?"

He debated how much to say, though he also needed to impress his senior partner if he had any hope of gaining the man's respect. He pointed at the location where Griese was discovered, then the second body. "Look at the distance between these two points. Given the timeframe, I think someone had to use a vehicle, which rules out Joachim."

Vogel agreed. "Unfortunately, there were scores of vehicles in the area doing bomb assessment damage, searching for Griese, delivering goods. But you're right, it does, I believe, rule out Joachim."

Stadler sat at his desk opposite Vogel. "So, what did the colonel have to say?"

"Not a lot, though what he did say was important and should help us at least narrow things down a bit."

"Who's this Frida girl?"

"His daughter."

"Huh?"

"His daughter. She died about six years ago in a car accident."

His eyes narrowed. "Why is that such a big secret?"

"They tried to protect the boys from being traumatized by the death, so they told them she had gone away. The boys eventually forgot her, then when Joachim saw the family photo, all the memories came flooding back and he panicked. He was already upset about what Griese had done, so when Griese told him he knew their secret, he snapped and fired the shot."

"What *had* Griese done?"

"He allowed General Graf to exit his vehicle early and step on his lady friend's dress. I guess it was a little embarrassing, and the general wasn't too pleased. He ordered Griese transferred to the Eastern Front."

"Sheesh, remind me never to cross him."

"Tell me about it."

"So, this was all over the fact they kept it secret that they had a daughter who died?"

"From Joachim's standpoint, yes. He thought they were going to lose everything for some reason, then thought he had killed Griese when he fired blindly. When he was found, he was in a panic, probably thought the only way he could salvage his future was to turn his parents in, so insisted on talking to Himmler himself."

"Are you going to report it?"

"Report what? That a family lost a daughter to a car accident years ago, and lied to their children about it to save them the pain of losing a sister? I hardly think that warrants being reported."

Stadler frowned. "I suppose not." He folded his arms. "Then where do we stand? I mean, are we any closer to figuring out who killed Griese?"

"Beyond knowing that Joachim couldn't be involved, not really."

He took a chance. "What about the colonel?"

"What about him?"

"Well, he would have access to a car. Couldn't he be the shooter?"

"He could, though what would be his motive to cover it up? As far as everyone was concerned, Griese had taken a shot at the party, and would likely be executed minutes after being captured. He could just shoot him, claim he had delivered justice, and then been congratulated on a job well done. No, I think the colonel is the least likely suspect here."

"So, we're no closer than we were last night."

"No, though questions are slowly getting answered. The next step is to get a list of everyone who was on the grounds last night, and start to eliminate them one by one. The colonel is supposed to get it to me today."

"Are we sure it was someone from the household?"

"Not completely, but remember, we still have the matter of the small-caliber weapon. Joachim shot Griese in the ear, dropped it, and now it's missing. Griese was then grazed by a small-caliber bullet, and the neighbors heard the shot. It's likely the same weapon. That means it has to be someone from the residence. It's simply not believable that an unrelated party came to the residence, picked up the weapon, then found Griese, shot him, then decided he had to make everyone think another person was Griese."

Stadler shook his head. "That part still makes no sense to me. Are we still working under the assumption that the reason the killer did this was because he needed the body found? *A* body found?"

Vogel nodded. "I am unless you can think of a better reason."

He frowned. "This is giving me a headache."

Vogel chuckled. "Me too. Now, I'm going to put together my notes while they're still fresh, then I'm going home. My wife will kill me if I miss my dinner tonight. I suggest you get some rest and stay close to your phone in case there's a break in the case."

"I think I'll sleep here, just in case that list comes in."

"Suit yourself, just don't do anything with it. We don't want to piss off the wrong person with indelicate questions."

Stadler regarded his partner.

No, you *wouldn't, would you?*

Central Records

Berlin, Nazi Germany

Hoffman entered the main lobby of Central Records, tucking his hat under his arm as he strode toward reception, his crisp black uniform sending any civilians in his path scurrying out of his way, sending a surge of energy through his system.

He loved the fear in their eyes.

It meant power.

And power was intoxicating. Addicting. And every chance he had to exercise it, it left him craving more. With each promotion, with each rung of the ladder he managed to climb, he gained more of what he sought, and realized why those in command had created the system they had.

They were drunk on the power.

And he wanted in.

Someday, he would be a colonel like Konrad, perhaps even a general like Graf. Dare he dream of being a Reichsführer like Himmler himself?

The power would be godlike. Men like the Führer, like Himmler, like Göring, like Goebbels. They were demigods that walked the face of the earth, the power they wielded unlike anything before seen by mankind.

It had to go to one's head.

Every morning when he put on his uniform and stared at himself in the mirror, he felt the adrenaline rush, he felt the pride surge. He could accomplish anything with this uniform, with the SS emblazoned on his collar, a symbol so misunderstood by so many, for they weren't the letter S at all, but Armanen Runes, the single lightning bolt representing the letter S in the 18 character alphabet handed down by the Norse God Odin, and the symbol for Victory. Their use now was so tied to the SS, so ingrained in German society, that even modern typewriters had been modified to add a key for the double lightning bolts so the proper honor could be afforded them, rather than the incorrect letter S being typed twice.

He loved his life.

He loved his Reich.

And he loved to serve.

Loyalty was everything, whether to the Party, the SS, the Reich, or to his commanding officer. Colonel Konrad was a fine commander, and he would do his utmost to serve him and serve him well.

That was why he was here, now, wasting his time picking up something that should be delivered, for he didn't trust anyone here to treat the matter with the attention it was due.

"Can I help you, Captain?"

"Hoffman. Here to see Zimmer."

"Is he expecting you?"

"He better be."

The woman blanched slightly. "One moment, please." She picked up her phone and after a few moments of whispering, she hung up. She pointed to a set of stairs to her left. "Top of the stairs, your first left. Room two-oh-four."

He bowed his head crisply and snapped his heels together, then headed up the stairs. He found 204 and opened the door without knocking, startling the man inside, his eyes widening with fear at the sight of the Hugo Boss produced uniform.

"Are you Zimmer?"

"Y-yes. You must be Captain Hoffman." The portly, sweaty man rose, wiping his brow with his hand then extending it for a handshake. Hoffman eyed it with disdain, the hand slowly retreating for a wipe against a pantleg. "I'm sorry." He grabbed two files from his desk. "I had copies made for you." He handed them over. "These are the two individuals in question. We're still trying to figure out what's going on."

Hoffman flipped through the pages of both files. "It would appear one was identified through fingerprints provided by a medical examiner, and the other by identity papers found on the body of a victim from the air raid last night?"

"Yes."

"Then isn't it obvious which one is the real Corporal Griese?"

Zimmer's eyes widened. "Oh, of course! It's obviously the one with the matching fingerprints."

"Then why the delay in officially notifying his commanding officer?"

Zimmer paled. "I'm sorry about that. Policy states situations like this must be resolved before any notification is made."

Hoffman frowned. "Then your policy is flawed."

"Of-of course it is." Zimmer paused. "Umm, will *you* be notifying his commanding officer, or should we?"

Hoffman shook his head in disgust. "I will be notifying Colonel Konrad, however you must properly notify the chain of command immediately that Corporal Griese is deceased. As to the other man, I couldn't care less about him."

"V-very well."

Hoffman headed for the door when Zimmer cleared his throat. "You said Colonel Konrad was his commanding officer?"

"Yes."

"It-it could be just a coincidence, but we had a request come in just a short while ago from the Kripo."

Hoffman turned. "What sort of request?"

"They wanted us to run the names Frida Konrad and Frida Baum."

"Baum?"

"Apparently Colonel Konrad's wife's maiden name."

Hoffman kept his expression emotionless. "And the Kripo requested this?"

"Yes. Urgently."

"Have you found anything yet?"

"No, but we're working on it."

"Keep me informed." He stared at Zimmer. "And tell no one that you told me."

"Y-yes, sir."

Konrad Residence

Berlin, Nazi Germany

"I heard a car leave, is he gone?"

Konrad nodded at his wife as he closed the inner doors to their bedchambers. He undid his collar and removed his jacket before sitting in his chair. "He is."

"And?"

He could see from her pale cheeks she must have been going through hell the entire time he was downstairs. He smiled. "It went well."

Her shoulders sagged. "What did he ask you?"

"As expected, he asked about Frida."

"What did you tell him?"

"In the end, the truth."

Her eyes shot wide. "You're not serious!"

"There was little choice. If I hadn't, I think he would have kept digging. By telling him who she was, and how she was special, he no longer has to dig for answers. After all, who would make up a story like that, a story that could get us all in serious trouble?"

"But can you trust him?"

Konrad nodded. "I think so. I sense he's an honorable man. He's just a police officer doing his duty, and a father who would do anything to protect his children, as I did."

"And what about Joachim? Did he ask about him?"

"I told him the truth there, as well. I told him Joachim saw a photo of his late sister, it triggered childhood memories that had him fearing for his future, he panicked, stole your weapon, wounded Griese, then ran away. I also told him about how I made it appear that Griese had been killed in the bombings, far enough from our home so no one could suspect Joachim had finished the job."

Her head sank to her chest as it shook. "You've told him too much!"

"Perhaps, but everything I told him was true, and he knows it. He won't be looking at us anymore. You know the dangers there if he does. If Graf caught wind of any of this, we'd be done for."

"Graf! Oh, how I hate that man. Is he still after us? How much time do we have left?"

Konrad checked his watch. "At least six hours. Hoffman should be at Central Records getting the files I need to prove Griese is dead. I'll take them to the general the moment I have them. He should be off our backs with time to spare."

"I'll breathe a little easier then, I suppose. With Joachim back and calming down, and with Graf satisfied with Griese's death, and that police officer perhaps leaving us alone now that you've explained our involvement, perhaps we might just make it through."

He smiled at her, trying to convey the confidence he lacked. "I believe we will."

She fidgeted for a moment. "I, umm, also took care of another matter that I…"

His eyes narrowed. "What is it?"

"I found something in the fireplace. When I was burning…things."

"What did you find?"

She stared at him, her eyes portraying the fear she had for both the question and the answer it might merit. "I found a piece of a uniform in there."

His head jerked back. "Uniform? What kind?"

"SS."

"Why would someone be burning an SS uniform?"

She paled slightly. "I was thinking it was Griese's. You said he was stripped naked. That means someone in this house—"

He smiled slightly, interrupting her. "Darling, I must confess something."

"What?"

"You know how I told you I found Griese's papers in his quarters?"

"Yes."

"Well, that's not true. I found his body when I went searching for Joachim the first time. I feared Joachim had shot him, so I hid the body. When I went out to find someone to plant his papers on, I actually retrieved them off his body. I realized that I couldn't just put the papers on some random corpse. It had to be someone with a matching uniform, or there'd be too many questions asked. And the likelihood of another SS corporal being killed was next to nothing, so I took his uniform. I'm sorry, I should have told you, but you had so much on your mind, and I didn't want to burden you with anything else."

Her eyes were wide and the relief on her face was clear. "Oh, thank God! I thought we had a spy in our midst!"

He chuckled. "Well, we probably do, though none involved in this, I assure you." He paused. "Though I do wonder why an SS uniform was burned. And in our own fireplace, nonetheless. Very odd. I'll ask Hoffman to look into it. I don't want my staff burning perfectly good uniforms."

"A good idea." She paused, returning to her fidgeting, something else clearly on her mind. "With all this time on my hands, I've been thinking about our previous conversation."

"We've had many, my darling."

She flashed him a quick look and a smile. "About leaving. About going into hiding."

He tensed. "Yes?"

"I'm not saying that's what we should do, at least not now, but we need to have a plan. A real plan. We need to be able to leave at a moment's notice and disappear. We can't risk the lives of our children in the hope that our secret will never be discovered."

He sighed. "You're right, of course. But let's worry about one crisis at a time. As soon as this is over, I'll give it some serious thought."

"You mean you'll consider it?"

He shook his head. "No, I agree we need a plan. I mean I'll give serious thought as to what exactly that plan should be. We'll need forged identity papers, travel permits, clothing, supplies, money. Everything set aside for when we pull the trigger on our leaving."

"Where would we go? You said your sister's place?"

He dismissed the idea with a wave of his hand. "Forget that. I was hasty with that idea, which is why you are correct. We need a proper plan. Everything depends on how much time we'd have. If I knew something was coming, I might be able to get us out of here a couple of days ahead of it, and that might be all we need, but I think we need to plan better." He regarded her, his chest aching with the idea. "I think you and the boys should go stay with my sister."

"But you just said—"

"Not permanently. The four of us traveling together is difficult. A woman and her two children might not be as conspicuous. If I got you out of the city, then arranged for papers to get you to the south of France, we could get you into Spain."

"What about Switzerland?"

"The border is too heavily guarded. We'd never get you near it. Spain, however, isn't as well guarded. If I could get you there, then join you, we could cross, perhaps with the help of partisans." He exhaled loudly. "It's just so insane to think about. The distances are just too large. And…"

"And?"

"And none of it will work, regardless."

"Why?"

"Joachim. As soon as he figured out what we were doing, he'd turn us in the first chance he had."

"What if he knew the entire truth?"

Konrad grunted. "He'd turn us in today."

Renata frowned. "You're right, of course. I love my son, but he's become a monster."

"His entire generation has."

"Our generation isn't much better."

"Our generation has been led astray by charisma and fear. In time, that will pass."

"Spoken by an SS colonel."

The words stung and she immediately sensed the hurt she had caused. "I'm sorry, dear, I meant it in jest."

He nodded. "I know, but…well, you know if I could change things, I would. But I had no choice. When you're approached by the SS and asked to join, you simply can't say no, not when you're in the Wehrmacht. If I had been civilian, perhaps I could have made excuses, but not as an officer in the Army."

She rose and walked over to him, kneeling at his feet. "I know, my love. You're too good a man to be part of this group of fanatics."

There was a knock at the outer door that had them both flinching. Renata rose and headed for her vanity while he answered the door.

It was Hoffman.

A smiling Hoffman waving two file folders. "I have the proof, sir!"

Relief swept through Konrad's body as he took the files, leafing through them, feigning ignorance. "So, there were two identified as Griese."

"Yes. One identified by fingerprints, the other by identity papers."

"And does Central Records have an explanation?"

"Not yet, though they are investigating."

"But they obviously agree that this one, the one with the fingerprints, is the correct Griese?"

"They have conceded that fact, yes, sir."

"Good. Then I will take this to the general. He will be very pleased to hear Corporal Griese has been found, and the Reich has been saved the expense of an execution." He smacked Hoffman's chest with the files. "Excellent work, Captain."

Hoffman swelled with pride. "Thank you, sir."

Konrad handed the files back. "Take these to my office. I'll be down in a minute."

Hoffman's heels clicked and he took the files before marching off, a spring in his step. Konrad returned to the bedchambers. "We have the proof we need. I'm going to go see the general now."

"Thank, God."

Konrad Residence

Berlin, Nazi Germany

Hoffman inspected himself in the full-length mirror on the back of his office door. With his commanding officer about to make an appearance, he wanted to be certain he was in perfect order after his outing. While the black uniforms of the SS were stunning, they were also unforgiving.

He brushed a speck of dust from his shoulder then stepped back to his desk, straightening the two file folders yet again. He let his eye roam the office, looking for anything out of place, anything crooked, anything that might reflect poorly on him, and by extension his CO and the SS, and, as expected, found nothing.

Everything was perfect, as it should be, his obsessive fastidiousness paying off.

Two raps on the door were followed immediately by its opening, Konrad stepping inside without waiting for an invitation. And none should have been expected. This was his house, and he was the commander.

Hoffman turned and snapped to attention. "Colonel."

"You have those files?"

Hoffman bowed slightly and clicked his heels before retrieving the two from the desk. He handed them to Konrad.

"I'm of two minds on these."

"Sir?"

"Do I inform General Graf that Griese is dead, and present the file we know to be true, and leave it at that? Or do I inform him of the second file as well, introducing confusion into the situation."

"I would think complete honesty would normally be best, especially with a man such as the general. Should he catch wind of any attempt at deception, it could prove…unfortunate."

Konrad grunted. "That's putting it mildly." He shook the files. "Yet one is obviously not Griese, therefore is merely a clerical error. I assume Central Records agrees?"

"Yes, sir."

"Then do I waste the general's valuable time on a clerical error? His concern is merely the whereabouts of Griese, whom we know is on a slab in the morgue."

"Yes, sir, I suppose so, sir."

Konrad eyed him. "You think I should inform the general of the entire situation."

Hoffman chose his words carefully. He respected the colonel immensely, and was honored every day to serve such a man. He considered him honest, loyal to the Reich, and a man who could be trusted to do what was best for everyone. Including his family. And his men. And that made everything he knew such a difficult burden to bear. It was clear Konrad had been struggling over the past 24 hours. The dinner party had been a disaster of biblical proportions, his son had gone missing, his wife was in a state, one of his staff was accused of an assassination attempt, and had now turned up dead in mysterious circumstances. Police had visited twice, and things were only going to get more difficult.

Konrad needed a confidante he could trust.

And that was him.

Yet how could he let him know?

"Well, not the *entire* situation, sir."

Konrad's eyes narrowed. "I'm not sure I know what you mean."

"I mean, share only what the general could find out on his own. Nothing more."

Konrad's head slowly bobbed then he held up the files. "Share the files, and nothing more. They tell everything officially known."

"Exactly."

Konrad sighed. "You're right, of course, Captain." He smacked him on the shoulder. "I always value your counsel. You're a good man."

Pride surged through Hoffman at the praise heaped upon him by this honorable man. "You honor me with your words, Colonel."

Konrad turned to leave then stopped. "Oh, one other thing. My wife found remnants of a uniform in the drawing room fireplace. Look into it, would you? I want to know who's burning uniforms rather than having them repaired."

Hoffman cleared his throat. "Umm, that was me, sir."

"You?"

"Yes, sir. I, umm, burned your uniform from last night."

Konrad's eyes widened slightly, and Hoffman was certain he had paled. "Why would you do such a thing?"

Hoffman had to tread carefully. "I feared…that the wrong people might begin to ask how it got soiled in the first place."

Konrad was definitely pale now. "Whatever do you mean?"

Hoffman thrust his chest out, squaring his shoulders. "I would prefer not to say."

"You'll tell me this instant!"

Hoffman's head fell. "I'm ashamed to speak of it."

Konrad relaxed slightly. "Tell me what's on your mind, Captain. The air needs to be cleared between us if you are to be my trusted man."

Hoffman nodded. "Very well, sir." He looked at his commander. "Sir, I'm ashamed to admit that I followed you last night."

Konrad stepped back, his hand reaching behind him for something to steady himself. "You…you did what?"

"When you left here to look for Joachim and Corporal Griese, I followed you."

Konrad sat and Hoffman did the same, not wanting to be staring down at his commanding officer in his vulnerable state. "Why would you do such a thing?"

"I was concerned for your safety, sir. Corporal Griese had just tried to kill someone at your party, an air raid had just begun, and with the state of things, I knew looters might be up to no good."

"Wh-what did you see?"

Hoffman stared at the floor. "I'm not sure."

"Captain."

He looked up, squaring his shoulders. "Very well, sir. I saw you confront Corporal Griese, then struggle for a weapon. It went off, then there were two more shots, one of which killed Griese. You dragged the body into an alleyway, then returned home."

"And that's all you saw?"

He nodded. "Yes, sir."

"And you kept this to yourself. Why?"

"You're my commanding officer, sir, and you did nothing wrong. Griese resisted, he was killed."

"Yet I didn't report the fact."

Hoffman glanced at the mirror. "I think we both know why, sir."

Konrad gripped the arms of his seat. "We do?"

"Yes, sir. We both know you didn't kill him."

SS Reich Main Security Office

Niederkirchner Straße, Berlin, Nazi Germany

"Cutting it close, Colonel."

Konrad nodded at General Graf. "Yes, sir. As you can see, there's been confusion at Central Records with one body being misidentified as Corporal Griese. That's why there was a delay in the notification."

Graf poured over the two files with more interest than Konrad had been hoping. The past hour had been a series of shocks, not the latest being Hoffman's revelation that he had seen the murder. The man was loyal, to a fault, and for now that loyalty was working for his family, but it could turn at any time.

It meant they had to begin planning their escape in earnest.

"It says here that your corporal was reported murdered by the coroner's office?"

"Yes, sir."

"And the other one was found dead from last night's air raid, with your corporal's identity papers?"

"Yes, sir."

"Do you have an explanation for this?"

He tensed. "I do not, sir. My aide visited Central Records personally, and they indicated they are working under the assumption it was a clerical error. They have launched an investigation."

"I should hope so. Perhaps the SS should take over and straighten things out over there."

"A capital idea, sir."

Graf grunted, pushed the files back toward him, then stared at him, causing Konrad's heart to pound. "So, who killed your corporal?"

Konrad's cheeks burned. "Sir?"

"According to the file he was found on Strausberger Street. That's nowhere near the bombings. How did he die? Who killed him?"

"I don't know, sir."

"Shouldn't a good commanding officer know how one of his men died?"

Konrad gulped. "Of course, sir. I've already spoken to the investigators from the Kripo, and they will be keeping me informed."

"Do they have any theories?"

"None they have made me aware of."

Graf grabbed his phone. "Very well. Keep me informed."

"Yes, sir." Konrad turned to leave and had made it all the way to the door when Graf stopped him.

"And what of your son?"

"He was found and returned home safely, sir."

"Good. Get your house in order, Colonel. You won't be given a second chance."

"Yes, sir."

Konrad left, and it wasn't until he reached his car and the relative privacy it granted him, that his entire body shook.

"Are you all right, sir?"

He glanced at his driver. "Yes. Just a chill, probably from being out last night looking for Joachim. I'll be fine."

"Where to?"

"Home."

"Yes, sir."

They pulled away from the imposing structure that housed the SS's top brass, and as soon as it was out of his sight, he felt slightly better. The meeting had gone as well as could be expected. Graf was off his back, though there would be no more chances. They had to leave the country, yet he had no idea how that could be possible with Joachim.

The boy was as devout a Nazi as Himmler.

What had him more concerned at the moment, was what to do with Hoffman. The fact was, there was nothing he *could* do with Hoffman. The man now had leverage over him. Leverage that would have been meaningless last night if he had simply told the truth immediately, but because he hadn't, he was now stuck with the lies he had told.

All to protect his wife and son.

When he had been made aware of his wife's discovery after the shooting, he had returned to the backyard and found the gun lying in the grass. He pocketed it to hide their involvement—if it had been found by Graf's men, there would have been no explaining how such a gun, preferred by ladies, would have been used in an assassination attempt. Suspicion would have fallen on his family for certain.

With the gun secure, he ran in the direction he had seen Griese flee. The bombs were pounding the city in the distance, and few were on the streets, those that were merely stragglers heading for the shelters. It was dark, the moon providing little light, and he was forced to rely on his ears.

And with few about, the heavy footfalls of a running man were easy to pick out.

Why Griese was still so close, he wasn't sure, though with his mind still piecing together the events of moments ago, he feared the corporal might be searching for Joachim.

For Joachim was the shooter, and Griese was the target.

Griese would be armed. If he found Joachim, he might kill the boy, or worse, bring him to the authorities as the shooter, and his son, in his current state of mind, might tell everything he knew.

It would be their end.

Griese had to be stopped, not only to protect Joachim, but to protect the entire family.

For Griese knew the truth.

He spotted a shadow dart across the street and took off in pursuit. He reached the crossroad and peered around the corner to find Griese standing in the middle of the road, looking in either direction. There was a loud crash behind him and he spun to see three men several houses down looting one of the more upscale homes in sight.

And rage filled his stomach.

Yet he had no time to deal with that.

Another set of footfalls echoed nearby, though he couldn't make out where they were coming from, the rows of apartments making it difficult to pinpoint anything.

Yet Griese still stood frozen, as if debating what he should do.

He's going to tell.

He crept toward him, almost reaching him when his foot slipped slightly on a patch of mud on the cobblestone.

Griese spun, his eyes bulging at the sight of his commanding officer.

"Sir! What are you doing here?"

Konrad squared his shoulders. "I could ask you the same thing, Corporal."

"I-I was looking for Joachim, sir."

"Why?"

"He, umm, he shot me, sir."

Konrad removed the weapon from his pocket. "With this?"

Griese's eyes widened. "Yes!"

"And when you found my son, what were you intending to do?"

"Bring him home, of course." Griese looked about. "Sir, he knows."

"He knows what?"

"He *knows*."

Konrad's chest tightened as the implications of what Griese was implying confirmed his wife's fears.

Griese knew their secret. Their terrible secret.

His finger slipped onto the trigger and he aimed it at Griese. "So, *you* know."

Griese raised his hands slightly. "I'm sorry, sir. I didn't mean to. It was an accident. You said to get your wife, and when she didn't answer the door, I went in and found her at her table with it. I didn't mean to! I swear!"

Konrad's heart ached at the boy's pleas. For he was a boy. Just three years ago, this young man would have been Joachim's age. How much growing up did a boy do in those three short years? Was he that much different than his son? Had he done anything wrong? He had stumbled upon a secret. A deadly secret. It wasn't a state secret that might demand imprisonment or death, it was a family secret.

Did this innocent man deserve to die for discovering it any more than they did for keeping it? If it was anyone's fault, it was theirs. And how were circumstances of birth anyone's fault? In a just society, they wouldn't be, but in today's Germany, they were. A society the furthest thing from just, dominated by paranoia and hate, with a lust for Aryan supremacy that wouldn't end until the entire world was under the thumb of the hate that emanated from the Reichstag.

And now this young man, this boy, was about to pay the ultimate price for merely being in the wrong place at the wrong time.

Because his wife had been careless.

He lowered the weapon slightly.

"This isn't your fault."

Griese sniffed, tears flowing freely. "I-I don't want to die, sir. I swear I'll tell no one."

Konrad's hand shook. "I know you would never tell anyone. You're a good boy. But this is my family." He sighed. "If only I had gone to get her myself."

"Please, sir. Let me return to my post. Transfer me if you have to." His eyes widened. "The Eastern Front! Send me there. I won't tell anyone, and I'll probably be dead by Christmas."

The sound of shoes scraping on the cobblestone behind Griese had Konrad leaning to get a better look. Suddenly Griese's hands darted out and grabbed for the gun. Konrad stepped back as the hands gripped his wrists. He squeezed the trigger and Griese yelped though kept going, bending Konrad's hand back painfully, causing the weapon to clatter to the ground. He reached for his sidearm but Griese delivered a kick to his midriff that had him doubled over, gasping for air. He looked up to see Griese draw his own weapon. Konrad lunged forward, grabbing for the man's arm.

A shot rang out, deafening, then another, farther away. Griese's eyes bulged and his chest surged forward as he fell toward Konrad. Konrad stepped aside, the young man collapsing to the ground, gasping for breath before falling silent. Konrad looked around, trying to find the shooter, yet only heard footfalls fading in the distance.

Who had saved him? And why hadn't they revealed themselves?

There could be only one reason.

They hadn't saved him. They had executed Griese.

It had to be Joachim.

He had to act fast. There was no way he could explain why Griese had been shot in the back if he was the one confronting the man. They would want to know who the second shooter was. They would eventually figure out Griese had been shot at the house because of the wound to his head inflicted by his son. Everyone at the house was accounted for except for Joachim.

Too many questions would be asked, and too much evidence remained.

No one could find Griese. Not yet, not until he had time to think.

He made sure he was alone, then dragged the body into a nearby alleyway. He covered his poor corporal in garbage, cringing at the disrespect. He retrieved his wife's gun, then made for his house, drawing his sidearm, not willing to risk anyone else in the shadows coming for him.

And when he reached his house to find his wife outside, hiding in the shadows, another horrid thought had occurred to him.

Perhaps it wasn't Joachim at all, but his wife.

And now, after all his efforts to keep his family out of it, it turned out that all along, Hoffman had known the truth.

At least some of it.

And he had no idea what to do about it. The list of staff and guests should be in the hands of the Kripo before the day was out, and once they started asking questions officially, would Hoffman maintain his silence? Would his duty to the Reich outweigh his duty to his commander?

He feared it would be the former.

That meant to save his family, he would either have to kill Hoffman, or somehow have the police solve the murder before they questioned his aide.

But how?

The two most likely murder suspects were Joachim or his wife.

Yet were they? There were looters in the area that night. Maybe one of them fired the fatal shot.

His jaw dropped.

Hoffman!

Hoffman had been there by his own admission. If he were in the shadows and witnessed everything, couldn't he be the one to have taken the shot? Joachim was definitely not the shooter. He was certain of that. Joachim was unarmed, and the likelihood of him finding a second weapon was nil.

His backup weapon.

It was in the bedroom, in plain sight. When Joachim had entered to steal his mother's weapon, he might have found the second weapon as well. He shook his head. No, that wouldn't make sense. Why take a .22 when a Luger was within reach?

But Hoffman would have had his sidearm. A Luger 9mm. The same type of caliber that had killed Griese, according to the police.

Could Hoffman be playing him?

It made so much more sense than the horrible theories playing out in his head over the past day. The very idea of Hoffman being involved had never entered his mind as he had always assumed his aide was at the house, seeing to the safety of his guests.

Was Hoffman the killer?

And if he was, could he somehow make the truth known to the police? Could they arrest him and solve his problem?

He chewed his cheek, thinking it through. What had Hoffman actually done? He had shot an assassin in a life or death struggle with his commanding officer. Was that a crime?

Yet if that were the case, why hadn't Hoffman shown himself?

He growled.

"Sir?"

He flinched at the sound of his driver. "Nothing, just thinking of all the paperwork I have on my desk."

Vogel Residence

Berlin, Nazi Germany

Vogel sat in his chair, his wife serving up tea to their guests sitting on the couch opposite them. His eyes became heavy and he drifted.

A swat on his arm startled him.

"Don't you dare fall asleep while we have guests!"

He grunted, shifting in his chair and taking his cup. "I'm sorry. I've been up since yesterday morning."

Their next-door neighbor, Hermann Lang, put his tea down. "Important case?"

"It's a murder!" called his wife from the kitchen.

Vogel grunted. "They usually are."

Erika shook her head. "I can't believe there are still murders at a time like this. If you want to kill, go kill the enemy! We're at war, for Heaven's sake."

Sofia took her seat. "What was it you said, darling? Cooks still cook, bakers still bake, and murderers still murder?"

He grunted. "It sounds like something I might say."

"Can you tell us anything?" asked Erika, leaning forward, clearly eager for any sordid details he might be willing to share.

"I'm afraid I can't discuss an active investigation."

Erika frowned and leaned back in her chair. "I suppose not." She turned her attention to Sofia. "So, when are the children coming back?"

"Tomorrow."

Vogel glanced over at a family photo sitting on a table at the far end of the room. It was taken near the river two years ago, just before the war had started.

A happy day.

His eyes narrowed at a thought, and he turned to Hermann. "Hermann, do you see that photo over there?"

Hermann looked at where he was pointing and nodded. "Of you and the family?"

"Yes. How did you know who was in it?"

Hermann's eyes narrowed. "What do mean? It's not you guys?"

"I'm not saying it isn't, I'm just asking how you knew. Can you actually see our faces?"

Hermann grunted, leaning toward the photo in his chair, shaving a few centimeters from the many meters. "I guess not. I just assumed, I suppose."

Vogel's head bobbed, his mind racing. "You just assumed." He leaned forward in his chair. "So, you can't see any of their features?"

Hermann shook his head.

"And you, Erika?"

"No, not really. Hair color, perhaps."

"So, if my daughter had a big scar on her face, or an oddly shaped nose, you couldn't tell?"

Erika's eyes narrowed as she gave him a look. "What an odd question!"

"Indeed," muttered his wife. "Wolfgang, what is this all about?"

But he wasn't listening to her anymore. To any of them. They were background noise to his racing mind as a piece of the puzzle fell out of place, a puzzle with so many pieces still missing, that anything that no longer fit stood out.

Glaringly.

What was it that Konrad had said? That Griese had caught his wife looking at the photo in her bedchambers? And he had seen her from the doorway, ducking away before she could spot him.

Yet she had.

It meant she had to have been seated with her back to him, otherwise she would have seen him immediately and said something. And the photo was kept in her vanity. Likely she would have taken it from wherever it was kept, and looked at it before putting it back. With the danger that photo represented, he couldn't imagine her strolling around the room with it.

She was likely near her vanity, which had to be across the room from the door, otherwise it would be on the same wall as the door, and she would have spotted Griese coming.

And the photo would have been facing away from him, so he couldn't have seen who was in it.

He smiled slightly.

The photo had to be a good distance across the room. Even at three meters, he would have seen it for a mere split second. And then even if he recognized it as the Konrad family, there was no way he could spot a child with the facial features Down Syndrome brought.

"There's no way he could have known their secret!"

Sofia groaned. "Oh no, he's no longer with us." She leaned toward her guests. "He gets like this when he makes a break in a case. He starts talking to himself."

Hermann chuckled. "Fascinating. When I'm operating a train, I talk to myself all the time. Can't say I've done it in front of anyone, though."

Vogel stared at them for a moment, his brain catching up to their conversation. "I'm so sorry, but you'll have to excuse me for a moment." He rose, not waiting for a response, and headed into the bedroom, closing the door behind him, the floorboards creaking under his feet as he paced the room.

If Griese couldn't see enough details in the photo to know Frida was handicapped, then what secret had he discovered? Why had he felt it necessary to retreat from the bedroom before fulfilling his orders? Why had he told Joachim that he knew the secret?

He smiled, turning and facing the mirror, staring at himself.

"He did know a secret."

He dropped onto the bed.

"A different secret."

That had to be it. Griese walked into the room, saw Konrad's wife doing something so disturbing it would cause him to rush out. But what was it she had been doing? Was it something inappropriate? Sexual?

He shook his head. Whatever it was, it was something Griese thought Joachim had discovered as well. And with the boy so upset, he probably realized the boy had *just* discovered it.

And Griese would know Konrad's wife was at the dinner party.

So, he probably assumed they had both seen the same thing, rather than overheard something.

Yet it couldn't be a photo. It had to be something else she kept in her bedchambers, something Joachim hadn't seen, for if Griese had seen it earlier, and it was indeed concerning, she would have absolutely taken care to hide it away properly.

Not just put it away in an unlocked drawer.

"But what can it be?"

There was a knock at the door before it opened and his wife poked her head in. "Darling, you're being rude to our guests."

He sighed. "I'm sorry." He followed her back into the living area and returned to his seat.

"Solved the case?" asked Hermann.

Vogel chuckled. "No, but I may have just had a breakthrough thanks to you."

Frida wasn't the secret. It was something else.

"Frida!"

He bolted for the phone.

Central Records

Berlin, Nazi Germany

Zimmer tugged as his shirt, pulling it off his sweat-soaked body. He had been running around the building all afternoon, applying as much pressure as he could to keep his staff working the phones, pouring over paperwork, trying to get the answers they needed.

And some were coming in.

After talking to the medical examiner, he had confirmed that indeed both bodies identified as Griese were connected. It was believed that the murderer of the real Griese had planted the identity papers on another body to throw the investigation off track.

This was all he needed to hear.

It was enough to let them officially correct the record, and the search was now on to determine who the man actually was, and Corporal Griese's name now only appeared on one file.

The record was correct, and the error hadn't been theirs. They were merely victims of the deception.

The paperwork had just been sent out to notify the corporal's chain of command, and all the proper departments of his death, so pay could be stopped, relatives notified, and the other myriad of bureaucratic nonsense that constituted a modern government could move forward.

He loved it. He loved paperwork. He loved every minute of his job.

Except when dealing with terrifying sorts such as Captain Hoffman.

Nothing struck fear in him more than the sight of the jet black uniform, though perhaps the leather trench coat of the Gestapo might. Either in one's office was never a good thing.

That was why, as soon as Hoffman had expressed an interest in the "Frida" search, he had redoubled their efforts, the tentacles of Central Records reaching out across the country to pull birth records, death records, hospital records. Anything that might have the two names they were searching for, anything that might link to the Konrad family.

There was a double-tap on his door then it pushed open and Ludwig, one of his clerks, entered. "I think I might have found something, but we just got a phone call."

"What about?"

"The police have told us to call off the name search. They said they've figured out who she is."

Zimmer sighed. Hoffman wouldn't be happy about that, but with the search canceled by the department originally requesting it, there was nothing he could do. If Hoffman wanted the information, he'd have to file a formal request.

SS or not.

He is not *going to like that.*

"Then I guess we can shelve it. Tell the staff."

"Fine, but, umm, I just got a hit, and I think you're going to want to see it."

Zimmer eyed the man then sighed, his curiosity winning out over the rule book. "What did you find?"

"Well, I decided to pull the colonel's file and track down every place he's lived since he was born. Quite the career he's had, so it's taken time. I was curious as to why they were asking us to search on his name and his wife's maiden name, so it had me thinking that maybe this Frida person wasn't just a relation, but maybe it was a child. *Their* child."

Zimmer's eyes narrowed. "His record shows two boys. Sixteen and ten."

"That's what the record shows, yes, but what if it was incomplete?"

"If it predated National Socialism, then it could be. What did you find?"

"Well, if we go from two years before they were married, just to take into account illegitimate children, then ignore the past fifteen years that he's been in the Wehrmacht and SS where they would have kept meticulous records, we have only one possibility. Their hometown of Offenburg."

Zimmer leaned forward, his heart rate picking up, a records search as exciting to him as the greatest mystery novel. "And?"

"And I found a birth record for a Frida Baum on April 14, 1925."

Zimmer fell back in his chair, folding his arms. "Unbelievable! But wait. Why Baum? Was the child a bastard?"

"That's just it. I talked to the administrator at the hospital that was listed, and he was there at the time. He actually remembers the Konrads because there were complications with the birth, and he swears they were married at the time."

Zimmer's eyes narrowed. "He remembers them after all these years? Surely there are plenty of complicated births."

"I asked him that. And you know what he said?"

"What?"

"He said he remembers because Konrad visited the hospital about six years ago, asking to see his daughter's file."

"Did he say why?"

"He doesn't remember."

"But he let him?"

"Yes."

Zimmer took a drink of his coffee. "You think the colonel changed his daughter's record to his wife's maiden name."

"Exactly. He wouldn't have been able to just destroy it, since the record would have been requested then would have had to be returned. I think he changed the surname on the record so it would be more difficult to trace the child back to him. We rarely conduct searches for children under the maiden name. Not for senior officers."

Ludwig was correct. The assumption was always that the children were legitimate when it came to officers. Especially SS senior officers.

His eyes narrowed. "But why would he not want us to find out he has a daughter?"

"Well, remember I said there were complications?"

Zimmer nodded.

"Well, the kid was mentally handicapped. Down Syndrome."

Zimmer's eyes shot wide. "No wonder he doesn't want anyone to know." He opened Konrad's file, pulled earlier in the day. "But he has two children. What happened to her?"

A shrug. "Could he be hiding her?"

"Impossible. An SS colonel? The vetting that would have been done? There's no way he's hiding her. Not these days."

"Maybe she's dead?"

"Could be. I don't know how long those children live with that. You don't see a lot of them around, especially now."

"You don't see a lot of people anymore."

Zimmer tensed. "Watch yourself."

Ludwig flushed. "Sorry. I don't know why I said that."

Zimmer dismissed the man's fears with a sweep of the hand. "Forget it. We all say the wrong things sometimes. We just need to be careful who we say them in front of."

"Thanks. Umm, what are we going to do with all this?"

"Officially, nothing. However, with it being a child covered under Aktion T4, we're obligated to report her, then let them investigate Konrad."

"I've got the birth records being sent here by phototeleautograph. We should have them shortly. I was told there was something I had to see on them."

"What?"

"He wouldn't say, not over the phone. He just said he was dutybound to report it."

Zimmer wiped the sweat from his brow. "Fine. Let me know when you've got it. I'll fill out the paperwork to report Frida *Baum* as a possible Aktion T4 candidate. Let them deal with it."

Ludwig left, closing the door behind him, leaving Zimmer alone with his thoughts.

Sometimes a successful search isn't as satisfying as one would hope.

If young Frida Baum wasn't already dead, she was about to be.

And it sickened him.

His eyes widened. Hoffman was Konrad's aide. That would mean he knew the man and his family intimately. If Frida were alive, then could he know the secret the family was hiding?

And if he did, what would he do to the supervisor at Central Records who had discovered their secret?

All blood drained from his face and his bladder let go as he slumped in his chair.

Kriminalpolizei Headquarters

Prinz-Albrecht Straße, Berlin, Nazi Germany

Stadler woke with a start, bolting upright in the bunkbed buried deep in the complex where officers took naps when it wasn't worth the time to go home then come back for a shift that would soon be starting. The life of a police officer was never nine-to-five.

Especially detectives.

He enjoyed it. In fact, he loved it. When his father had pushed him into the job, he hadn't been happy, though it was a relief to not go fight with his friends. The war had just started and was raging on two fronts, the death notices rolling in steadily for a while. As soon as he had graduated, his father had secured him the job, saving him from active duty.

For now.

Perhaps one day he might have to serve, but he doubted it. Europe was mostly secure, Russia would soon be defeated, and the English would be flying the Nazi flag at Buckingham Palace within a year. Then who was there to worry about? The Americans? They were burying their heads in the sand, which was perfect. Once Europe was secure, then Asia and Africa, Germany would have time to build the navy they needed to mount an invasion of the Americas. If he were at the table, planning the conquest with Hitler and the inner circle, he'd go through South America, then march northward, then when America turned its attention there, open a second front in Canada.

It would be easy with the massive resources afforded by the Reich's control of Europe, Asia, and Africa.

They'd be unstoppable, and eventually the war would be over, there would be peace with the Nazi flag fluttering over every former capital.

His chest swelled.

I can't wait for the day.

He rolled out of bed and freshened up before returning to his desk. An envelope was waiting for Vogel and he glanced at it. It was from Colonel Konrad's office. He sat down then opened it. It was a single page containing two columns of names, separated out into guests who were at the party, as well as staff and soldiers on the grounds during the time in question.

And there were scores of them.

This is going to take forever.

He took out a piece of paper and began jotting down the names he felt would need to be followed up with. Those who could have perhaps committed the murder. He eliminated all the guests. It was his understanding that all of them were in the bomb shelter during the air raid. He eliminated the female house staff, and the children except for Joachim, whom he still had lingering doubts about. It was still an extensive list, what with the soldiers regularly assigned to the post or brought in special for the night, and the large contingent of caterers and support staff tending to the twenty guests and two hosts.

It was a substantial affair.

I never would have thought it took so many people.

He had seen movies and newsreels portraying events such as this, and was always impressed when a long line of waiters would appear carrying trays, placing them in front of the guests, then with a flourish, they would all remove the covers simultaneously, revealing delicacies he could only taste in his dreams.

And if such a display took place last night, it would take 22.

Insanity.

Though judging from the extensive list, that might have been exactly what took place, and once done, how many would have actually been needed? Could one of them during their idle time have killed Griese? But what possible motive could they have had?

He shook his head, leaning back in his chair. It had to be someone normally at the residence, not someone brought in for the night. None of the catering staff would have had a weapon with them, and the soldiers wouldn't have left their posts. And if they had encountered Griese during the search for him, and subsequently shot him for whatever reason, there would have been no repercussions. He had just attempted to assassinate a senior officer, or so everyone thought at the time.

No, it couldn't be one of the soldiers brought in, nor the catering staff.

And that left a short list.

None of which were someone named Frida.

He eyed the phone. He wasn't certain how long it would take for any results to come back from his search request, but he had made it a priority request, and would have thought there'd at least be a progress report by now. He picked up the receiver, placing the call to Central Records, and was soon transferred to a supervisor.

"This is Zimmer."

"Hello, this is Kriminalassistent Otto Stadler, Kriminalpolizei. I put in a priority request earlier for two name searches. Frida Konrad and Frida Baum."

"Yes, yes. That request was canceled."

Stadler's eyes shot wide. "Excuse me? By whom?"

"I don't have the name in front of me, but it was one of your people. A kriminalinspektor if I remember correctly. Not long ago."

Stadler hung up the phone, his mind racing as he leaned back in his chair. Only two people here knew of the request. Him and Vogel, and Vogel was a kriminalinspektor. It had to be him.

But why?

Why would he cancel the name search? Yes, they now knew Frida was the colonel's deceased daughter, but why not confirm that? At this moment, they only had the man's word on it. And he wasn't entirely convinced that everything that had happened was related to a girl dead for six years.

Something else was going on.

Griese dying and Joachim fleeing all around the same time was simply too much of a coincidence. There was obviously a connection. If the boy had shot Griese in the ear then fled, then Griese went after him, where did Joachim get the weapon to shoot the corporal? It didn't make sense for him to have two weapons. Then who killed Griese? It had to be someone from the party, and why would they kill over something as trivial as a dead daughter they had kept secret?

And what kind of parents told their sons that their sister had gone away, then never spoke of her again?

That didn't make sense to him. Why would they want their daughter to be forgotten? Why no photos displayed proudly in her memory? Why was Frida a forbidden name in the Konrad household?

His eyes flared.

It was something *about* her that had to be forgotten.

He leaned forward and grabbed the phone, reaching Zimmer within seconds. "Reinstate that records search."

"Consider it done."

Central Records

Berlin, Nazi Germany

Zimmer hung up the phone with the Kripo detective, staring at Ludwig who stood in front of his desk, having just delivered the copy of the files sent from Offenburg.

Files that were shocking.

He stared at the incriminating page in front of him listing the birth of Frida Konrad, the birth parents listed plain as day. "I don't understand. He changed her surname on the official birth record. Why wouldn't he change this? This is more damning than anything!"

Ludwig dropped into a chair. "It's not the official record. It's a copy."

Zimmer looked up from the page. "A copy?"

"Yes. Remember how there were complications with the birth? That she had Down Syndrome? Well, they kept records of those. Anyone born with a birth defect had their files copied and sent to a research department at the university there. This is that copy."

"So, our colonel would never have known it existed."

"He couldn't have."

"And he would have gotten away with it too if it weren't for your digging."

Ludwig frowned. "I don't want the credit."

Zimmer eyed him. "Why? You did your job and you did it well."

"People are going to die because of this. I'd rather forget about it."

Zimmer nodded. It was a difficult thing. With Aktion T4 in place, Frida Konrad, if she were still alive, soon wouldn't be. But what they had uncovered by accident was something far worse.

And would result in the death of an entire family, if the rumors were true.

"What are you going to do?" asked Ludwig.

"My duty. I have no choice. If I didn't, and the man who provided you these records found out, he could report me, then it would be me who was executed, along with the Konrad family."

Ludwig rose. "This…this…" His shoulders slumped. "Can I go now?"

"Go. And don't feel guilty about doing your job. You and I both know we have no choice in these matters anymore."

Ludwig left the room, leaving Zimmer with the grim task of making the official notifications. The paperwork was one thing. The paperwork didn't scare him.

It was the phone calls.

The police were waiting for the information.

But so was Captain Hoffman.

A man he feared knew the secret his commanding officer was hiding, and might kill to protect the family. A father. Two sons.

And a Jewish mother.

Kriminalpolizei Headquarters

Prinz-Albrecht Straße, Berlin, Nazi Germany

Desk Sergeant Abel sauntered through the large room containing dozens of detectives and the empty desks of dozens more. He had never wanted to be one. He had always preferred the uniform he still wore proudly. But a badly broken knee after a fight with a perp, had left him unable to perform his duties.

Relegating him to a desk.

He missed it, though there was some satisfaction at manning that desk at the front, being the first point of contact for the public needing help, for helping coordinate the efforts of the hundreds that worked here.

He was respected.

He was needed.

He was useful.

Vogel's phone rang, something it had been doing the entire length of his walk through the office, and no one seemed keen to answer it. He picked it up. "Kriminalinspektor Vogel's desk. Sergeant Abel speaking."

"This is Zimmer from Central Records. May I speak with him, please?"

"I'm sorry, he's not here at the moment. Can I take a message?"

"Yes. Tell him we have the information on the names he asked us to search. Please have him call me at his earliest convenience."

"Hey, Sergeant, who are you talking to?"

Abel glanced behind him to see Stadler returning to his desk with a fresh cup of coffee. "One moment, please, his partner just returned." He handed the receiver to Stadler. "Central Records for you."

The young man's eyes shot wide and he grabbed the phone. "Yes?"

Abel continued his stroll back to the front desk, exchanging pleasantries with the others as he passed. Before he could reach the door, Stadler rushed past him, struggling to put his jacket on. "What's the rush, son?"

"That bastard knew! He had to have!"

"Who knew what?"

"Vogel! He had to have known!"

Stadler blasted through the doors, leaving a dozen puzzled fellow officers in his wake. Abel returned to his desk and picked up the phone.

Vogel Residence

Berlin, Nazi Germany

When the evening was finally over, Vogel would be willing to admit to his wife that he had a good time. Hermann and Erika were good people, but he was exhausted. He had managed to squeeze in about two hours of sleep in the past two days, and was fading fast.

He needed them to leave.

Now.

The phone rang and a surge of energy gave him a slight second wind. He excused himself and answered it. "This is Vogel."

"Hello, sir, this is Sergeant Abel. Something's happened that I think you should know about."

Vogel tensed. "What's that?"

"Well, it's about your young partner. You see, your phone was ringing, so I answered it. It was someone from Central Records saying they had the info you were looking for on a name search."

Vogel's heart raced. "But I canceled that search."

"I can't speak to that, however Stadler returned to his desk, took the call, then raced out of here very angry, claiming you had known something all along."

Vogel held his tongue. Central Records must have found out Frida Konrad had Down Syndrome. Yet he couldn't be certain. "Did he say what it was I was supposed to have known?"

Abel chuckled. "No, sir, but he was pretty upset."

"Any idea where he went?"

"Sorry, sir, no idea."

"Very well, thanks for letting me know." He hung up the phone and immediately called Zimmer at Central Records. "This is Vogel. What did you find on Frida Konrad?"

"Oh, your partner didn't tell you?"

"I'm not at the station."

"Well, we found out several things, actually. Frida Konrad is the daughter of the colonel and his wife, though his official record doesn't indicate he has a daughter, which is odd in itself."

"What else did you find?"

"Well, this is where it gets disturbing. It would appear that the daughter was born with a condition called Down Syndrome. I'm not sure if you're familiar—"

Vogel's heart rate picked up some more. Stadler now knew the secret, and was obviously assuming, correctly, that he knew as well. "I am. Go on."

"Well, we also discovered that he altered the birth records to show his wife's maiden name as the surname on the record. He was obviously trying to hide the fact he had a handicapped daughter."

"A reasonable assumption."

"Yes, yes."

"Have the records sent to my office. I'll review them later. Good—"

"Oh, Detective, there's more."

A wave of trepidation washed over him, his skin crawling with goosebumps. "What?"

"Something most disturbing that I'll be reporting momentarily."

"And that is?"

"Well, the birth records indicate the parents' religion, and these show that Mrs. Konrad is Jewish."

Vogel's pulse hammered in his ears at the revelation. It was something that had never occurred to him, though his young partner had suggested it with no evidence. He had been operating under the assumption the secret was Frida's condition, but when he had realized Griese couldn't possibly have known, and that there must be another secret, the wife being Jewish wasn't even on the map.

And once it was reported, they were all dead.

"Who have you told?"

"Your partner, and the colonel's aide, Captain Hoffman."

Vogel gripped the doorframe. "Why would you tell him? That was a Kripo request!"

"I-I'm sorry, sir, but he was here on another matter, and I made the mistake of mentioning your search when I heard who he worked for. I-I couldn't say no. He's SS!"

Vogel hung up and immediately called Konrad's residence, praying Hoffman didn't answer.

"Colonel Konrad."

"Sir, this is Kriminalinspektor Vogel. They know! Hoffman knows! You have to get out of there immediately!"

There was a pause, but when the response came, there was little doubt the colonel knew exactly what he was talking about. "What…do they know?"

"About your wife." He glanced at the forgotten room behind him, his wife and two guests staring at him, riveted. "About where she…used to worship."

"I see. Thank you."

The line went dead and Vogel hung up the phone, turning to the others.

"I have to go. If Stadler calls, tell him I went to arrest the Konrads."

Konrad Residence

Berlin, Nazi Germany

Hoffman sat at his desk, stunned. The phone call he had received only minutes ago was shocking, and so completely unexpected, he wasn't sure how to react.

Though that didn't last long.

Rage.

Disgust.

To think he had served a colonel who had married a filthy Jew was so revolting, his mouth filled with bile at the thought he had shared space with her and her half-breed children. He had been loyal to a man who would introduce impurities into the Aryan race by lying about the genetics of his own children.

It was unthinkable.

It was intolerable.

It was a crime of unimaginable proportions.

Griese must have discovered their secret!

The thought had him incensed. To think that an SS corporal was murdered to hide the fact the colonel's wife was a Jew was unforgivable.

Justice had to be delivered.

He rose and straightened his uniform, inspecting himself in the mirror before fitting his cap firmly in place, regarding the skull and crossbones on the band that meant so much.

This would disgrace him. This would set his career back for years, perhaps permanently. How could he ever live down the fact he had served a Jew-lover and not known it?

He drew his Luger from its holster and confirmed it was loaded.

This ends today, with the reclamation of my honor.

He stepped out into the hall and headed for Konrad's office. It was empty save a maid straightening up. "Where is he?"

"I believe he went to check on his wife."

Hoffman strode toward the stairs, his weapon held tightly at his side.

Konrad rushed into the bedroom, locking the door behind him. "We have to leave, now!"

Renata emerged from the bedchambers but he pushed past her, opening the safe. "What's going on? You're scaring me."

"They know!"

"What do you mean?"

He twisted his head to look at her. "They *know!*"

She turned ashen, collapsing onto the bed. "H-how?"

"Does it matter?" He pulled all of the money he had been setting aside for such an occasion, and shoved it into a small bag he kept in the safe, along with several ounces of gold and silver, and some family jewelry inherited from his grandmother. "Pack a bag with just the essentials for two days. I'll tell the boys to pack for a camping trip."

She didn't budge, instead sitting on the edge of the bed, shaking. He grabbed her by the shoulders and shook her.

"Snap out of it!"

She flinched then stared at him. "I'm fine. Go, get the boys ready." She rose and sprang into action. He placed the bag of money on the bed as he tried to figure out what to do beyond getting out of the house. If Hoffman knew, they might be doomed. He would have called Graf's office and notified him immediately to save his career, then would likely be about to arrest them himself.

He paused at the door, fearing what might be on the other side. He drew his sidearm and readied it, then unlocked the door, his ear pressed against it.

He heard nothing.

He slowly opened the door, peering down the hallway, seeing no one. He went to Joachim's room and opened the door, finding the poor boy sitting on his bed, reading. "We're leaving in five minutes. Pack a bag for camping, then go help your brother. Understood?"

Joachim scrambled from the bed. "Why? What's going on?"

He couldn't tell him the truth. The boy was still recovering from the shock of learning about his sister and her condition. To tell him he was half-Jewish, and that people were coming to arrest them because of it, would be devastating.

And right now, he needed the boy as cooperative as possible.

"Your mother is in danger. We have to leave now or they'll kill her."

Joachim's eyes widened. "Who?"

"Bad people." Konrad pointed at the large chest at the foot of the boy's bed containing his Hitler Youth gear. "Pack your backpack, now, then help your brother. Five minutes."

"Yes, sir!"

Konrad stepped back into the hall and gasped as he saw his bedroom door slowly close.

Hoffman!

He rushed back down the hall when his wife screamed.

En route to Konrad Residence

Berlin, Nazi Germany

Vogel floored the accelerator as he raced toward the Konrad residence. He was closer to their home than headquarters, but he wasn't sure how much of a head start Stadler had. He had to beat him there, just in case the Konrads hadn't left in time. Yet he still didn't know why. What was he going to do? Officially, he had to arrest them all and report it. If they didn't leave before he got there, he'd have no choice.

They were dead whether he or Stadler arrived first.

He punched the steering wheel. He hated his country. He hated what it had become. Did he love Jews? No. Nobody did, at least none that he knew. Yet did that mean they deserved to be treated the way they had been under National Socialism? He had heard the rumors, the reports of the camps, of the shootings, of the mass murders. He had dismissed them at first, yet there were so many stories told, at least some had to be true.

Did Konrad deserve to die because he had fallen in love with, and married, a Jewish woman when it was legal to do so at the time? Did their children deserve to die simply because they had been born to a Jewish mother? Did she, because she was born to Jewish parents?

The answer was obvious.

No.

But how could he prevent it? There was nothing he could do. He was powerless. If he interfered, he'd be shot. His wife and children could face the same fate as the Konrads, and if not, their lives would certainly be destroyed by his death or imprisonment.

Yet he had to do something.

They have to get out of the city. Out of the country.

The country was huge now, for it was no longer a country. It was an empire. They couldn't head east because that was where the Eastern Front was. They couldn't head north to the coast, because it was too tightly controlled, and west was the same. They'd never get a boat to England.

That left south.

The Swiss border was impenetrable without the proper papers, and farther south to the Mediterranean or the Adriatic was equally unrealistic. Spain? It too was a ridiculous distance, especially for four people with no papers, with the entire nation's security apparatus searching for them.

There was nowhere for them to run to.

"They need to be smuggled out."

His eyes widened as he careened around a corner, fists shaken at him by startled pedestrians.

"Smuggled out. That's *exactly* what they need."

And he knew exactly who could do it.

For a price.

It went against everything he stood for as a police officer, though as a man, a moral man, he could see no alternative. He had to get to the Konrads before they left.

Otherwise he might never see them again.

Alive.

Konrad Residence

Berlin, Nazi Germany

Konrad sprinted toward the door, shoving it open to find Hoffman advancing on the bedroom. He could hear his wife's cries on the other side of the wall, her terror clear.

"Captain!"

Hoffman spun toward him, his weapon extended. Konrad raised his own and squeezed the trigger.

Nothing.

It was jammed.

He sprung forward, grabbing Hoffman by the wrist and forcing the gun toward the ceiling, trying to break the man's grip. Hoffman kneed him in the gut and he doubled over, gasping for breath, his grip broken.

Hoffman pressed the gun against Konrad's forehead. "I'm going to kill you, you filthy Jew-lover! Then I'm going to kill that Jewess of a wife, then your half-breed children!" He spat in Konrad's face. "I can't believe I served under a man like you. You make me sick."

"You don't have to do this."

Hoffman's chin rose slightly to the right as a sneer spread. "Yes, I do. As would any good, loyal German." He dropped his gaze, staring directly into Konrad's eyes. "Burn in hell, traitor."

A shot rang out and Konrad flinched, as did Hoffman, his eyes bulging before blood sputtered from his lips. He dropped to his knees, the gun pressed against Konrad's forehead slipping down his face as the hand holding it went limp.

Someone screamed.

Konrad stared at Hoffman's lifeless body, now in a heap on the floor, then at his wife standing in the doorway, his spare weapon in her hand, still aimed at his captain.

And the scream continued.

But it wasn't from her.

He turned to see Joachim standing in the doorway, his eyes wide, with Maximilian beside him, his mouth open, the high-pitched wail continuing.

"Maximilian! Stop!"

The little mouth snapped shut. Footfalls could be heard pounding up the stairs.

They had little time.

Konrad rushed forward and grabbed the gun from his wife's hands, pushing her into the bedroom and beckoning his children to follow. He slammed the door shut as the first of the guards arrived.

"Sir, are you—"

The man froze, his eyes bulging at the sight of the captain, dead, a pool of blood flowing on the area rug he had been standing upon.

"He attacked my wife for some reason. Call the police and General Graf's office. Tell them what has happened. I'm going to take my wife and children to the hospital."

Heels clicked. "Yes, sir!"

He opened the inner door to the bedroom then immediately closed it after entering. He held a finger to his lips. "Now, everyone remain calm. We're going to go for a little drive, understood?"

Maximilian's eyes were still saucers, but he nodded.

Joachim was staring at his mother. "You're a Jew?"

The disdain was obvious and heartbreaking.

She nodded. "Yes. And so are you and your brother." She reached out for him and he recoiled as if her hand were the head of a snake.

"Don't touch me, you filthy Jew!"

Konrad smacked Joachim across the face. "Don't you *ever* talk to your mother like that!"

Joachim's eyes welled with tears, never before having been hit by either of his parents. He said nothing.

"Now, people are on their way here. We are all going to die if we don't leave." He jabbed a finger at Joachim. "And that includes you. Whether you like it or not, you are as Jewish as your mother in their eyes."

"I don't want to be a Jew!"

"You don't have a choice. But tell me, now that you know you are, are you any different?"

"What do you mean?"

Konrad hauled him in front of the mirror. "Look at yourself. Are you any different? Is your nose bigger than yesterday? Is it crooked? Is your hair different? Your ears?" He shook him. "Well?"

Joachim sobbed, tears racing down his cheeks. "No!"

"But shouldn't you look different? Isn't that what all the hate tells us? That Jews look different? That you can spot a Jew easily? That if you see one you should report it?" He spun Joachim around to face him, and stared deep in his eyes. "Do you think I'm a good man?"

"Y-yes."

"Would a good man love your mother, and love you, if it were wrong?"

"I-I guess not."

"Then realize that you are the same young man you were five minutes ago before you knew. Strong, intelligent, and a good person. Do you love your mother?"

His head dropped. "Yes."

"Then hug her."

He rushed around Konrad and into Renata's arms. "I'm sorry, Mother! I'm sorry!"

Tires squealed outside and Konrad's heart leaped into his throat. He rushed out onto the balcony and sighed with relief at the sight of Vogel climbing out. Vogel spotted him and beckoned them down with a wave of his arm.

"One minute!" Konrad went back inside. "Let's go. No time for bags." He grabbed the bag of cash and valuables off the bed and herded everyone out of the bedroom and past the guards collected in the hallway. "We're going to the hospital now."

"Yes, sir. Do you require an escort?"

"No need. We're not in any danger now."

They rushed down the stairs then outside.

"Point your gun at me, Colonel."

Konrad stared at Vogel. "What?"

"Just do it!" hissed the man.

Konrad aimed his weapon at the detective.

"Everyone in the car, quickly," said Vogel, holding the rear door open. Renata and the children climbed in, then Vogel rounded the car, his hands up. He sat in the driver's seat and started the car. Konrad took the passenger seat and pulled the door shut, and moments later they were off the property, mixed in with the light evening traffic.

"What was that all about?"

Vogel turned a corner. "I'll explain later. Is everyone all right?"

Konrad glanced back at the others. "As good as could be expected, I suppose." He eyed Vogel. "Why are you helping us?"

"Because it's the right thing to do."

"Won't you get in trouble?"

"Only if we're caught."

Konrad frowned. "I assume you have a plan?"

"That depends. Do you have money?"

Konrad shook the bag. "Yes."

"A lot?"

"Enough."

"Then yes, I have a plan."

"What?"

"First things first. I want to know what happened last night. Everything."

Konrad Residence

Berlin, Nazi Germany

Stadler skidded to a halt in front of the entrance to the Konrad residence. Guards were rushing around, and two directed weapons at him. He raised his hands.

"I'm Kriminalassistent Stadler, Kriminalpolizei. Where is your commanding officer?"

The weapons lowered as he produced his ID. "They've gone to the hospital. There was an incident."

"What happened?"

The guard appeared puzzled. "You're not here because of it?"

"What do you mean?"

"There's been a shooting. A man is dead. You were called. Isn't that why you're here?"

Stadler shook his head. "No, I'm here to arrest Colonel Konrad and his family."

The man's eyes widened. "On what charge?"

"The colonel for harboring Jews, and the rest of his family for being Jews."

Shocked looks were exchanged by everyone within earshot.

"You said they went to the hospital. Why?"

"Captain Hoffman attacked the colonel's wife. The colonel shot him."

Stadler rushed up the steps. "Show me!"

Moments later he was in the Konrads' bedchambers, confirming Hoffman was indeed dead, shot in the back.

Just like Griese.

"You said the colonel shot Hoffman?"

"Yes."

"But he was shot in the back. Why not the front?"

The man shrugged. "I wouldn't know, sir. I only heard the shot."

"You said they left. I assume in their car? I'll need its—"

"No, sir, someone else arrived and took them. In fact…"

Stadler eyed the man. "In fact what? Out with it!"

"Well, it was odd, sir. The colonel held a weapon on the man and forced him to take them."

Stadler tensed. "Who was it?"

"I don't know his name, sir, but I saw you come here with him earlier today."

Vogel!

But why would he be here? He was supposed to be at home. "I need a phone."

"Yes, sir." He was led to one and he called Vogel's home. Sofia answered. "Can I speak to Wolfgang?"

"He's not here, Otto. He told me to tell you he was going to arrest the Konrads. Do you know what that means?"

"I do. Thank you." He hung up, not sure what to do. He had been certain Vogel knew the truth about the Konrads, yet if he did, why would he have been coming here to arrest them?

It could be a ruse.

He chewed his lip. It was a possibility, but if that were the case, why had Konrad held a gun on Vogel and forced him to drive them?

Maybe Vogel didn't know. Maybe he was innocent.

Stadler's eyes widened. Vogel *was* innocent, and had just been kidnapped by a murderer with nothing to lose.

He picked up the phone.

Berlin, Nazi Germany

"Perhaps *I* should explain."

All eyes turned to Renata in the back seat, and she pointed at the road ahead. "Please keep your eyes on the road, Detective, you're driving my children."

Vogel complied, adjusting his mirror so he could make eye contact, no doubt to try and determine whether what she was about to say was the truth.

"You know something about what happened?" he asked.

"I do." She sighed, closing her eyes, replaying the events of last night. "When the shot was fired and the glass shattered, I knew immediately by the sound of the weapon that it might be mine. Instead of joining the others as they were sent into the bomb shelter, I went upstairs and discovered the drawer to my vanity open. The gun was gone, the family photo with Frida was out, and Joachim's dagger was on the floor. I screamed."

Konrad twisted in his seat. "That's when I was about to pursue Corporal Griese. Instead, I ran upstairs to see what was wrong."

"Exactly. After we agreed that Joachim must have shot at Griese, I told you about the corporal walking in on me while looking at my family's Torah. It was foolish of me to have it out, especially with so many guests arriving, but I was feeling guilty for what was about to happen. I was Jewish, we were in a house confiscated from a Jewish family, and we were about to entertain a bunch of Nazis who were responsible for it. I just wanted to say a prayer and beg forgiveness."

Vogel glanced at her in the mirror. "Where is the Torah now?"

"I burned it earlier today."

Her husband reached out and squeezed her hand. "I'm so sorry I made you do that."

She smiled weakly. "It's not your fault. You were right, it was too dangerous to have."

Vogel spun his hand, urging her on. "Then what happened."

Konrad continued. "I went outside, found my wife's gun where Joachim had dropped it, then went to look for Griese and Joachim. I knew Joachim would be upset about remembering Frida, but I also knew Griese had found out my wife was Jewish. He had to be found."

"So, you went out to kill him?"

Konrad sighed. "To be honest, I don't know. Part of me wanted to kill him. The poor boy was dead already. General Graf thought he had just tried to assassinate one of the guests, so he would probably be executed. I feared he might try to save his life by telling our secret. I had to protect my wife and children. I didn't care what happened to me, but I couldn't let anything happen to them."

"So, you killed him?"

Konrad shook his head. "No, I didn't."

"You told me you found his body, though."

"That's not entirely true."

The car slowed slightly. "What do you mean?"

Konrad frowned. "Here's the truth. All of it. I found Griese, but he was alive."

Vogel's eyes shot wide. "He was alive? *And* you didn't kill him?"

Konrad shook his head. "No. I confronted him. He said he was looking for Joachim because my son had shot him. He said he wanted to bring him home. I showed him the gun, and he confirmed it was the one Joachim had used. There was a sound behind him. I moved to see who was there and he grabbed for the weapon. There was a struggle, the weapon went off, but I don't think I hit him."

"Actually, you grazed his shoulder."

"Oh. Well, the weapon fell to the ground, I reached for my sidearm, but he kicked me and drew his first. I grabbed for it, he fired, missing me, but then there was another shot. Someone shot him in the back."

"Who?"

"I have no idea."

"It was me."

The car swerved back and forth several times as Vogel tried to regain control after the shock of her revelation. Her husband stared at her wide-eyed, as did the boys.

Konrad spoke first. "*You* shot him?"

She nodded, her eyes welling with tears, her shoulders shaking as her heart threatened to pound out of her chest. She had been living with the guilt for almost a full day, and every moment had been agony. As time passed, and suspicion kept shifting, she had thought she might get away with it, yet part of her had wanted to confess the entire time, to end the lie they had been living.

But she couldn't.

It wasn't just her life she was protecting.

"As soon as you left the room, I took your backup weapon and followed you. I lost you for a bit because you were too fast for me, but I found you again, talking to Griese. When you started to struggle with him, I thought he might kill you, so I shot him, then ran back home. You came back a few minutes later, said nothing about what had happened, so I decided to not tell you what I had done. I returned your weapon when you went to see the guests off safely, then have been trying to figure out what to do since."

Vogel looked at her in the mirror. "That was quite the shot, Mrs. Konrad. You expect me to believe you made it?"

"I'm an expert shot, Detective. When I was younger, I used to compete, but once we started a family, I gave it up. Now I only shoot for fun, and even that I haven't done in years."

Vogel's head slowly bobbed. "Then that's that."

Konrad shook his head. "No, it isn't. I shot him."

Vogel glared at him. "Don't give me that garbage. Your wife just confessed, and now you're going to try and confuse the issue?"

"No, my love, I did it. You don't have to try and cover for me."

Konrad squeezed her hand. "No, you're both misunderstanding me. What I'm saying is that the official record must show *I* killed him. If we're caught, and they find out she killed an SS soldier, *and* that she's Jewish, they'll torture her until the end of time. *I* have to be the one they think killed Griese."

Vogel regarded him for a moment, then glanced at her in the mirror. "You're right. They'd show no mercy." He sighed. "Very well, you killed Griese. Let's just hope no one saw what really happened."

"Captain Hoffman saw what happened, though he didn't see who actually fired the fatal shot. He just saw the struggle, then me hiding the body."

Vogel frowned. "That's going to be a problem."

"Not really. Hoffman is dead."

"What?"

"It happened just before you arrived."

"Did you kill him because he knew you were lying about Griese?"

"No, not at all. He found out my wife was Jewish because of a records search your people initiated, and was going to kill her and the children. There was a struggle…"

"And I shot him."

Vogel stared at her once again, his eyes wide for a moment. "In the back, no doubt?"

She smiled slightly, dipping her head. "As a matter of fact…"

"So, Hoffman is dead, and we're assuming no one else saw anything, since no one else has come forward yet. We should be safe sticking with the story that you killed Griese, but I'm hoping that won't matter."

Konrad's eyes narrowed. "That's right. You said you had a plan. What is it?"

"I'm taking you to a man I know. A bad man. One we've been trying to arrest for some time, but he's well protected because of his father."

"Who's his father?"

"It doesn't matter. He's high up in the Party, and the less you know the better."

"Why are you taking us to such a man?"

"Because he can get you all out of Germany, and I can't."

Konrad Residence

Berlin, Nazi Germany

Stadler stepped aside as a squad of SS soldiers rushed down the hallway, a general he assumed was Graf bringing up the rear. The imposing figure assessed and dismissed him with a glance before entering the room and staring at the dead captain.

"Who shot him?"

Stadler stepped forward. "Apparently Colonel Konrad did, sir. He claimed the captain attacked Mrs. Konrad, and he defended her."

"You're telling me that a trained SS soldier like Captain Hoffman allowed himself to be shot in the back?"

Stadler paled, Graf taking the suggestion personally, as if the very idea were an affront to his own sense of honor. "I-I don't know, sir. I can only go by what I was told."

"Are you the Kripo detective in charge?"

This is one of those times Vogel was talking about.

"At the moment."

"Then aren't you a trained investigator? Shouldn't you be able to tell me something useful here?"

"I-I'm just a junior detective. My partner, my senior partner, was kidnapped at gunpoint by Colonel Konrad."

Graf grunted. "Interesting, that. I wonder where the colonel thinks he's going. Every checkpoint in the city has been notified. The airport, trainyards, ports. He won't be getting anywhere. Not with a woman and two children."

"A Jewish woman."

Graf froze, his head turning slowly toward Stadler, his eyes boring into the young detective's. "Excuse me?"

"We just found out that she's a Jew."

Graf's lip curled as rage and disgust filled his eyes. "I shared a meal with that woman, and you're telling me she's a filthy Jew!"

Stadler cringed at the revulsion, something he had never seen nor experienced before. He was no fan of the Jews, and was happy to see them being forced out of his country, yet couldn't say any had ever wronged him. This man, however, clearly had a level of hatred for them far deeper than Stadler had ever seen before. "Yes, sir," he murmured.

Graf drew a deep, slow breath, his eyes widening with a zealotry that would fit well within the inner circle of the Party. "Tear this place apart. Colonel Konrad is obviously a traitor. If there's any evidence here that he was passing information on to the enemy, I want to know. And I want every man, woman, and child that has interacted with any of them in the past year picked up and interrogated. If there's one, then there's a dozen.

They're like rats, and I want them all found." He jabbed a finger at Stadler. "This is our investigation now. The Kriminalpolizei are no longer welcome here."

Gruber Residence

Berlin, Nazi Germany

Vogel's skin crawled as he stepped inside the opulent residence of Felix Gruber, one of the most villainous scum to have taken up residence in Berlin since the rise of National Socialism. His father was close friends with Himmler, one of the original members of the Party, and untouchable by anyone but the Führer himself.

And that meant so was the son.

The Kriminalpolizei were desperate to bust Gruber, but after several careers were ended, and two officers disappeared permanently, no one dared touch the man. Instead, they focused on his associates.

Which gave Gruber carte blanche to do whatever he wanted.

And judging from their surroundings, business was good.

The human smuggling business.

"He'll see you now."

Vogel acknowledged one of Gruber's henchman then turned to Konrad. "Stay here. I'll be back shortly."

"Do you trust this man?" asked Konrad, his voice low.

"Not at all. But what alternative do we have?"

Konrad frowned, but nodded. "Very well." He handed over the bag of money and valuables. "Let's hope this is enough."

Vogel entered the inner sanctum, the rotund Gruber sitting behind an ornate desk, half a dozen of his men occupying the periphery, holster bulges prominent. Vogel opened his jacket, revealing his own. "Do you want to disarm me?"

Gruber chuckled. "Believe me, Kriminalinspektor Vogel, I doubt you could best all of my men." He waved his hand. "Please, keep your weapon."

Vogel placed the bag on the blotter in front of Gruber. "I have need of your services."

Gruber ignored the bag. "*You*, a detective with the Kripo, have need of *my* services?"

"I'm not here officially. You know that. I have a family that needs to get out of Germany. To Spain then eventually America."

Gruber roared with laughter, his men joining in. "Is that all?" He flicked a wrist at the bag. "You'd need a potato sack of money for that."

"Then forget America. Just get them to Spain. They can figure out the rest."

Gruber sighed. "Who are they to you?"

"Does it matter? You've never been very discriminating before."

Gruber jabbed the air with his cigar. "Don't be rude, Wolfgang. It doesn't become you."

Vogel sighed. "I'm sorry. The situation is urgent. The SS is probably already locking down the city to find them. I need them out of the city within the hour, then in Spain as quickly as possible."

"Why Spain?"

"You have an alternative?"

"Switzerland seems to be a popular destination." Gruber leaned forward and opened the bag, rummaging through it with a frown. "Well, Switzerland is a little too rich for this sum. Spain it is."

"Then we have a deal?"

Gruber nodded. "We have a deal." He directed his cigar at Vogel. "But the next time I need a favor, you owe me."

Vogel's chest tightened. He was doing a deal with the Devil to save four innocent people. He just prayed whatever favor he was asked in the future didn't tip the scales of justice too far. "Understood."

"Then get out of here."

Vogel rose and rejoined Konrad and his family. "We have a deal. These people are going to take you to Spain, then the rest is up to you, understood?"

Konrad shook his head. "I still don't understand why you're doing this."

Vogel regarded Renata and then the children, all terrified, all innocent. "Because this isn't my Germany, and because of that, one day, I'll be executed, and when I'm before God, I want to be able to say I tried my best to do the right thing when I had the chance." He extended a hand and Konrad took it.

"How can I ever repay you?"

"Survive, Colonel. Survive."

Two men entered the room. "We have to go, now."

Renata rushed into Vogel's arms and hugged him. "Thank you so much for this, Detective. You're a good man."

"You're welcome."

The family was led out of the room, and Vogel said a silent prayer for their safety. Unfortunately, for all he knew, Gruber was delivering them to Gestapo headquarters.

He would never know.

He stepped back into Gruber's office.

The man glared at him. "Now what?"

"I need another favor."

Anhalter Bahnhof

Friedrichshain-Kreuzberg, Berlin, Nazi Germany

Vogel flinched as he woke, his head immediately pounding in agony. His eyes burned, and it took a moment for him to regain his bearings. He was in his car, seated behind the wheel.

And the back of his head throbbed like it was ready to give birth to something horrible.

Someone rapped against the window and he jerked away as a flashlight shone into his eyes. He held up a hand to block the glare.

"Open up!" shouted someone. "Police!"

Vogel sighed then rolled down the window. "Just a second. I'm Kriminalinspektor Vogel. Let me get my ID."

"Vogel?" The flashlight beam dropped. "Half the city is looking for you."

Vogel showed him his ID then opened the door, stumbling as he took his first steps.

"Are you all right?"

Vogel shook his head, immediately regretting it. "No, that bastard coldcocked me as soon as we got here. What time is it?"

"It's almost midnight. The call went out hours ago to find you." The officer's eyes narrowed. "You better sit back down, you don't look well." He turned and shouted at someone. "Get the station medic out here. And call it in. Let headquarters know we've found Vogel!"

"Right away!"

Vogel sat back in the driver's seat, gingerly touching the back of his head where Gruber's man had knocked him out with the butt of a pistol. It was the favor he had asked of Gruber, a favor he would pay the price for later, but a favor that he hoped would save his life. For the story he had to convince the others of, was that he had been kidnapped at gunpoint and taken here, where he was then knocked out.

There was nothing he could have done to prevent Konrad from leaving.

And by having Gruber's men assault him here, at the train station, the authorities would hopefully waste their time searching every train that had left here in the past several hours, rather than focusing on roadblocks and checkpoints.

It was a brilliant plan.

If it worked.

Two medics with a stretcher sprinted toward them, and after a quick assessment, he was horizontal and being carried into the small infirmary at the train station. In less than half an hour, there was a knock at the door, Stadler standing there appearing relieved.

"Are you all right?"

Vogel grunted. "I'll live. Concussion, apparently."

"Who hit you?"

"Konrad. He forced me to drive them here then hit me in the back of the head with his gun. I just woke up a little while ago."

"You're lucky to be alive. You know he killed Captain Hoffman?"

Vogel shook his head then winced. "No."

Stadler shifted uncomfortably from one foot to the other. "Umm, why were you there?"

"To arrest him, of course. Sergeant Abel at the station called me at home, told me you had left there in a huff after talking to someone at Central Records. I called them, they told me what they had found out about Mrs. Konrad, and I headed over there to arrest them all. Obviously, Konrad killed Griese to hide their secret. They were lying to us all along about everything."

Stadler shook his head. "Bastards. This is why you can't trust Jews."

Vogel bit his tongue. "Have they caught them?"

"No, but half the country is out looking for them. We'll find them in short order, I'm sure. Nobody betrays the Fatherland and gets away with it."

"Let's hope."

Stadler leaned against another bed. "So, did they say anything to you?"

"Not much, though the colonel did confess to killing Griese to hide their secret. The wife and kids had no idea what was going on."

Stadler grunted. "That doesn't matter. She's a Jew and they're both half Jew, so they'll be sent east."

Vogel cringed at the thought, and again prayed for their safe deliverance.

Stadler shrugged. "You know, for a moment there, I thought you were helping them."

Vogel gave him a look. "Why the hell would you think that?"

"Well, you've been acting kind of strange, and you called off the records search for Frida."

He sighed. "I only did that because we knew who she was, and it was irrelevant. I figured out that Griese couldn't have seen the photo from where he was in the room, so I knew that whatever it was he had seen had nothing to do with her." He gave his partner a smile, hoping to convince him that the final thread he was pulling at was nothing worth paying attention to. "I'm glad you reinstated it though, otherwise we never would have found out she was Jewish. I just wish he hadn't got the jump on me. I would have liked to have arrested him for the murder. I think he would have confessed to try and save his family."

Stadler laughed, and Vogel's stomach churned. "He could confess all he wanted, it wouldn't help. They would have been processed like all the others. Once we catch them, it won't change a thing. If anything, they've made things worse for themselves." He folded his arms, staring at his partner. "What do you want to do now? General Graf has taken over the investigation, and says we're no longer welcome."

Vogel sat up and swung his feet to the floor. "I don't know about you, but I'm going home to sleep for at least two days. I'll do the paperwork when and if I wake up."

Stadler chuckled. "Good idea. And maybe by then they'll have been captured, and we can close this case properly."

Approaching the Spanish Border

Vichy France

It had been a long, hard, terrifying journey, especially for the children. It had been days that were so uncomfortable at times, it felt like weeks. Shuttled from one town to the next, sleeping in barns and cellars, meager meals, little chances for the niceties they were accustomed to.

They were animals, and smelled as bad as the pigs they were now hidden under.

It was supposed to be their final leg of the trip.

And their most dangerous.

"Everyone remain completely quiet until I say so, understood?"

Slivers of light shone from overhead through the slats of the bed of the truck, and the bulbous bodies of the pigs, but it was enough for him to see three heads nodding.

"Now, everyone put their hands over their mouths, just in case.

Hands slapped in place, including his wife's.

Shouts erupted outside and the truck shuddered to a halt, muffled words exchanged before the engine shut off. The farmer driving them was supposed to be a local, a man who regularly crossed the border into neutral Spain.

And secretly a member of the French Resistance.

The truck shook as someone climbed into the bed, the pigs squealing as they were shoved aside, whoever it was clearly searching for hidden cargo. He stared above and could see the shadow of the soldier overhead. He reached into his pocket, gripping his wife's weapon, the only thing he had to defend themselves.

Yet it would be useless against a well-armed border unit.

He released his grip and instead found the small bundle in his pocket, a bundle he had retrieved from his office desk the moment he received the phone call from Vogel telling him that Hoffman knew their secret.

Their final solution to the problem.

He pulled it out and began to unfold it as the shouts continued outside, the guards agitated about something, everything in French, a language he now regretted not learning.

He had chosen English.

The search continued overhead, and he heard muffled gasps as one of the floorboards overhead lifted partially at the front of the truck. Eyes bulged and he held a finger to his lips, then finished unfolding the paper containing the cyanide pills he had acquired for just such an occasion.

They were about to be captured, and that could never happen.

He handed two pills to his wife, and he could see the tears flowing down her cheeks as she took them. The boys had no idea what was about to happen, and they couldn't know. He didn't want their final moments to be filled with the knowledge their own parents had killed them. More shouting from outside and the truck rocked again as the floorboard snapped back in place with a loud crack, one of the pigs having shifted and stepped on it. Cursing erupted, somebody in pain, a finger probably pinched.

He held a pill out for Maximilian. "Candy!" he whispered, and the boy's eyes brightened. His heart was pounding now as the rush of blood filled his ears. He was about to kill his family, to murder all that he loved, to save them from a fate far worse than death.

He would burn in Hell for eternity for what he was about to do.

And he was fine with that.

As long as they lived on in the Heaven he knew was there waiting for them.

The engine suddenly roared to life and his eyes widened as he reached out and enveloped his wife's hand with his own, gripping it tightly, the pills meant to prevent their suffering trapped within. The gears protested a bad shift, then they lurched forward, slowly picking up speed on the bumpy road.

He held his breath, as he was certain they all were, and a few minutes later someone knocked on the metal door of the truck several times.

"Welcome to Spain!"

His shoulders shook with relief as all the stress of the past days released. He let go of his wife's hand then threw his pills toward the back of the truck, his wife smiling then doing the same.

They were free.

They had made it.

All thanks to one man who had done the right thing, despite the risk to himself.

Kriminalinspektor Wolfgang Vogel.

THE END

ACKNOWLEDGMENTS

This book deals with difficult subject matter, including the treatment of Jews and the handicapped by the Nazis. There are characters with hateful views, and there are some who are not bad people, who expressed thoughts that don't fit in with our modern times. This book must be read with the understanding that it takes place almost 80 years ago, when things were very much different. It makes me wonder how people 80 years in the future will think about things we do and say today, and will they feel we were backward.

This book has been a dream of mine to write for many years. I introduced the character of Wolfgang Vogel in my novel James Acton #20: The Nazi's Engineer. That book was very well received, and it gave me the confidence to eventually try this novel. I hope you think it turned out well.

As usual, there are people to thank. My dad for all the research, Brent Richards for some weapons info, and, as always, my wife, daughter, and mother, as well as the proofing and launch teams.

To those who have not already done so, please visit my website at www.jrobertkennedy.com then sign up for the Insider's Club to be notified of new book releases. Your email address will never be shared or sold, and you'll only receive the occasional email from me, as I don't have time to spam you!

Thank you once again for reading.